T0120718

The Plan

Christianity on Trial

Miles R. Wilson

WestBow Press books may be ordered through booksellers or by contacting:

WestBow Press
A Division of Thomas Nelson & Zondervan
1663 Liberty Drive
Bloomington, IN 47403
www.westbowpress.com
844-714-3454

ISBN: 978-1-6642-6559-2 (sc)
ISBN: 978-1-6642-6560-8 (e)

Print information available on the last page.

WestBow Press rev. date: 6/2/2022

Dedicated to the brave citizens of Ukraine.
May God be with you.

Other book from Miles R. Wilson:

Don't Cry For Me Emma © 2020 Westbow Press

Reviews:

-*Wilson's prose is smooth and exact*...Kirkus Reviews

From previous book by Miles R. Wilson,
Don't Cry For Me Emma ©2020

December 28th, Conclusion

The small chapel was nearly empty. With no family, there were few mourners. Heather and Ben had accompanied Emma. Abigail Redgrave made a point to be present; her affection for this child was evident. Fred Patterson sat quietly near the front staring at the wooden cross on the wall. He had a solemn look about him. A couple of the nurses who had become very attached to Gabriella were in attendance, and even Doctor De Rosa made time to bid farewell to his former patient.

The minister spoke eloquently about the faith of a child, in reference to the scripture in Mark 10:15 – "Assuredly, I say to you, whoever does not receive the kingdom of God as a little child will by no means enter it." ***

Emma, surprising even herself, delivered the eulogy, speaking of the influence that Gabriella had on her life. Those in attendance listened attentively as the teen, struggling to keep her composure, spoke of Gabriella's positive outlook on life.

The funeral concluded with a local soloist presenting a powerful rendition of *Nearer My God to Thee.*

After the service, there were several hugs, and then the small crowd quietly filed out of the chapel into the frigid December day.

As Emma sat silently in the back seat of her mother's SUV

on their drive home, the snow began to fall; lightly at first, then growing in intensity. She stared out of the vehicle's window at the driving precipitation, causing her mind to flash back to that fateful night in October…the night that changed her life forever.

Suddenly, she thought, the '*Plan*' was beginning to make sense.

The End

Introduction

We live in an age in which our world is embroiled in strife that shatters us to the core; an age when our entire planet seems to be coming apart at the seams.

This book attempts to provide a glimpse into events that may occur in the not too distant future in our world; events that may challenge many people's core beliefs.

A future is coming in which so many of society's long-held beliefs may be cast aside to make way for a 'new world'.

I ask that you read this book with a mind that is open and ready to be challenged; a mind that is willing to consider possibilities that you never dreamed of.

M.R.W.

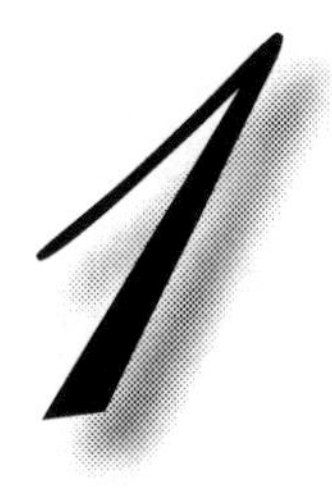

Monday, June 8

The driving rain pummeled her SUV as Emma Collins nervously drove through the tempestuous night. Her wipers struggled to keep up with the torrents of water cascading over her windshield. Emma was uneasy driving at night at the best of times, and tonight was proving to be the worst of times. Her out-of-town meeting with a new client had lasted longer than she would have liked, resulting in her delayed departure. She had hoped to beat the weather, but it was not to be on this night. She whispered to herself in frustration, "I should have left earlier and missed all of this."

Emma's mind was filled with the evening's events. Thoughts swirled around in her head as she tried to make sense of her meeting. *Did it go well tonight?* She wondered as she navigated the slick, winding road. *Did I say the right things? Was I too forceful? Was I forceful enough?* She continued to mentally dissect her meeting with this potentially significant client.

As Emma continued her late-night trek home, the storm intensified, now with blinding flashes of lightning, followed by deafening claps of thunder. She strained to focus on the road in front of her.

Suddenly, a fierce lightning bolt illuminated the sky, resulting in a large oak limb crashing to the ground only meters in front of Emma's SUV. Her immediate reaction was to swerve to avoid a collision with the fallen limb. As Emma pulled the steering wheel, her right front tire caught the rain-drenched shoulder of the road and sent her vehicle over an embankment. The SUV rolled violently twice and came to rest on its roof ten meters below.

Emma was dazed but remained conscious. She was upside down, held in by her seatbelt. The SUV was severely damaged, making it impossible for Emma to reach the release button on her belt. She struggled to grasp the button when her biggest fear was realized…the smell of leaking gasoline! *Oh, no!* She thought as she again grappled with the seatbelt. *Maybe the rain will prevent a fire or explosion.* Emma was trying hard to control her emotions and not panic! *Lord, please help!*

"Hello!" The sound was of an unfamiliar voice. Emma wondered if she was dreaming. *Who could possibly be way out here on this night?*

"Hello!" The voice was closer this time. "Anyone in there?"

"Yes," was the feeble reply. "I can't undo my seatbelt."

"Are you alright, Miss?" asked a bearded man as he peered into the overturned vehicle.

"I can't reach the seatbelt release," cried Emma.

The bearded man shone a flashlight into Emma's vehicle. "I see what you mean. Let me see if I can reach it. He struggled to find the release latch through the shattered window. What's your name?"

"Emma."

"Alright, Emma, let's get you out of here. I don't like the smell of that gasoline." He positioned the flashlight so that he could see properly and then the bearded man held the release latch with one hand and placed his other hand underneath Emma's head. "Okay. Emma, I have the release. You are going to feel a bit of a drop. Ready?"

"Yes, please hurry."

"Alright, here we go." The bearded man pressed the release and did his best to cushion Emma's slight drop.

Emma groaned as she came to rest on her shoulders with her neck in an awkward position. The bearded man gently took hold of her and pulled her from the wreck. He wasted no time in picking her up carefully and carrying her well away from the smashed vehicle.

By this time, Emma was losing consciousness.

"Stay with me, Emma. I have called 911, and help is on the way," said the bearded man in a comforting tone. He removed his heavy raincoat and covered the young woman as best he could. The weather was unforgiving and Emma began to shiver as she lay on the rain-soaked ground. "It will not be long. Stay with me, Emma."

The scene was almost straight out of a movie. Moments after pulling Emma from the vehicle, her SUV erupted into flames. Emma turned her head as she lay on the ground and gazed at the inferno. She quickly offered a word of thanks.

The fire was short-lived as the heavy rain pounded down and extinguished it within a few minutes. Emma thought she could hear the faint sound of a siren in the distance as she drifted into unconsciousness.

†††

"Hello," said Heather as she picked up her phone.

"Hello, Mrs., Collins?"

"Yes it is."

"This is Officer Max Bonner of the Ontario Provincial Police."

Heather's heart skipped a beat. "Yes?" she said, as her voice cracked.

"Do you have a daughter named Emma?"

Heather started to have difficulty breathing. "What happened?"

"Your daughter was involved in a single vehicle accident earlier this evening."

"What? Is she alright?" Heather could feel herself starting to panic.

"She's not seriously injured. Her life is not in danger, Mrs. Collins."

"I'll catch the next flight to Toronto," said Heather, trying not to lose control.

"I'll give you the number of the hospital where Emma was taken," offered Officer Bonner compassionately. "She's at Mercy Hospital." He gave her the number, and also his cell number. Please call me if there is anything that the Ontario police can do for you."

"Thank you so much, Officer," said Heather as she regained her composure.

"You're very welcome. Mrs. Collins. And remember to call if we can be of service."

"Thank you again, Officer." Heather pressed 'end' and gently placed her phone on her kitchen counter. Her mind started to fill with memories of that dreadful evening all those years ago in Regina. The night she received the call from the hospital telling her that Emma had been in an accident. *God, I pray that Emma is not badly injured. Hold her close, Lord and take care of her.*

Heather picked up her phone and punched in the number of Mercy Hospital.

†††

Emma's head throbbed as she awoke in unfamiliar surroundings. She looked around and quickly realized that she was in a hospital bed.

"Good morning, Emma. Glad you're back with us," said a young cheerful nurse.

"Where am I?" croaked Emma.

"You are in Mercy Hospital in Toronto," replied the nurse. "You were in a car accident last night."

"Yeah, I sort of remember," said Emma softly as she strained to recall the events from the previous evening. "What's wrong with me?"

"I'll have Doctor Levine come by to talk to you," said the nurse as she smiled warmly and left the room. "We contacted your mother last night. We noticed you had her listed as next of kin. She said she will call you today and that she would fly out to Toronto to see you."

"I'll call her when I am a little more with it," said Emma.

"Good morning, Emma," said Doctor Levine as he entered the room. "I'm Doctor Samuel Levine. You had a bit of a rough go of it last night, I see."

Emma forced a slight smile of acknowledgment.

"Well, the good news is that we can't find anything seriously wrong with you. You'll be sore for a while, but you should be fine with a little rest," assured the physician as he checked her vitals. "Everything seems good. I'd like to keep you today for observation. You should be able to go home tomorrow. Now, there are a couple of police officers here who would just like your help in filling out their report. Are you alright to talk to them?"

"Yeah, I'm fine, and thank you, Doctor," replied Emma as she began to feel a little better.

"Okay, I'll tell them you'll see them," said the doctor, and then promptly left the room.

A few moments later, two provincial police officers entered and introduced themselves. "I'm Officer Jacobson, and this is Officer Mercier. We just need to ask you a few questions to finish our report. Do you feel up to it?"

Emma nodded her head.

"Okay," said Jacobson. "It will only take a few minutes. Now, do you remember what caused you to go off the road?"

"Yes," said Emma. "Lightning hit a tree in front of me, causing a large limb to fall onto the road. I tried to swerve and must have caught the soft shoulder and went over."

"So, you were able to get out, alright?" asked Mercier.

"Uh, no, actually, I couldn't release my seatbelt. That's when that man showed up."

"What man?" asked Mercier.

"I didn't get his name, but he was able to free me and pull me from the vehicle before it caught fire."

"That's strange," said Jacobson, "because there was no one there but you when the paramedics arrived."

"He was a man, probably in his sixties, with a beard."

"He must have called 911," added Mercier. "Did he say anything else?"

"Not really, he put his coat over me and talked to me for a while. I would have died if he hadn't shown up. I don't remember much more than that."

"Alright, thank you for your time. If we need anything else, we will get hold of you," said Jacobson. With that, the two officers exited the room.

Emma lay back on her hospital bed and reflected on the harrowing evening that had almost been her last. *Who was that man? Where did he come from? Where did he go? Thank God he was there!*

†††

After about thirty minutes, Emma asked for a glass of orange juice, which she gulped down. Feeling that her head had cleared enough, she grabbed her phone from her bedside table where hospital staff had left it. She punched in her mother's number.

"Emma? Is that you, honey?"

"Hi, Mom. Yeah, it's me."

"Oh, honey, what happened? Are you alright?"

Emma recounted the events of last evening as best that she could remember them, including the mystery man.

"Oh, dear, you could have been killed! Thank the Lord that that man showed up. I will be on the next flight to Toronto."

"I'm fine, Mom, really. I'll be back at work in a day or two, anyway. Tyrell and I are so busy; I can't afford to be off."

"But you were just in a serious car accident, Emma," said Heather.

"I'll be fine, and besides, I'd rather you and Ben come for a visit in the fall. I'll try to take a couple of days off when you are here. The two of you can check out the sites of the big city," said Emma, trying to sound upbeat.

"Well, it goes against my better judgement, but if that's what you want," said Heather. The mother and daughter talked for a few more minutes, and then said their goodbyes, promising to talk again soon.

Tuesday, June 9

Emma spent a long day in the hospital, resting her aches and pains. She felt that every muscle in her body had been stretched to the limit, and then some. Once her mind had cleared, she reached for her phone and punched in the number of her long time friend and law associate, Tyrell Lewis.

"Where you been, girl? I've been trying to phone you," said the voice on the other end.

"Sorry, I was in a bit of an accident last night."

"What!?" bellowed Tyrell. "What kind of accident? Where are you?"

"I'm at Mercy Hospital. I had a car accident."

"Be there in thirty. Don't go anywhere," said Tyrell. He hit 'end', grabbed his jacket, and ran for the door.

"Where am I going to go?" joked Emma as she winced at the sharp pain in her chest.

Emma laid back and thought about her good friend Tyrell. Tyrell was Emma's associate and soon to be a partner at the law firm. They had met in university and had been close ever since. They had long ago agreed to keep their relationship platonic, as not to complicate it. She was comfortable sharing her innermost thoughts with Tyrell, knowing that they had total trust in one another.

True to his word, Tyrell entered Emma's room twenty-nine minutes later. "Girl, what did you do?" he cried in mock admonishment as he drew close to the bed and clutched her hand.

"I was driving home last night from the meeting with a new client when that storm hit. It was bad. A tree in front of me was struck by lightning, and a huge limb came down right in front of me. I swerved and caught the soft shoulder and was...gone."

"Girl, you could have been killed!"

"You don't know how close I came. I was pinned upside down in my SUV, and I couldn't press the release on my seatbelt. There was the smell of gasoline leaking, and I thought I would die. Then, out of nowhere, a man showed up and was able to free me and carry me away from the vehicle before it caught fire."

"Who was he?" asked Tyrell.

"That's the thing. I didn't get his name, and he just disappeared before the ambulance and police showed up. He must have called 911. I have no idea who he was. All I know is that he had a beard, and he saved my life."

"Woe, can I give you a hug?" said Tyrell with a smile.

"Gently," answered Emma.

The two friends embraced and talked for a while longer about the mystery man, and details of the accident.

"I'll call your insurance company and get the ball rolling on your claim. You'll need a rental vehicle also. I'll take care of it."

'Thanks, a million, Tyrell. You're a good friend."

"We aim to please," said Tyrell with a smile. "Also, Maggie would like you to call her later if you feel up to it. She's concerned about you."

"I'll do that," said Emma.

"Okay, I'll get going on this stuff, and let you get some rest. Call you later." Tyrell gently squeezed Emma's hand, gave her a big smile, and exited.

Emma reached for her phone and pressed the 'call' button beside Maggie Barnett's name.

Maggie had been Emma's faithful secretary ever since her law office first opened. Emma often wondered how she could ever manage without Maggie Barnett, looking after things at the office. She felt truly blessed to have such dedicated people as Tyrell and Maggie as employees and friends. Emma took a moment and contemplated how much her life had changed since her youthful years in Regina, Saskatchewan.

Wednesday, June 10

Emma awoke the next morning, feeling like she was back with the living. She had a few aches and pains, but for the most part, felt quite well. Doctor Levine stopped by and examined her once again.

"Alright, you are set to go. Just take it easy for a few days. Your body has had quite a jolt, but you should be fine," said the doctor.

"Thank you, Doctor," replied Emma, happy with the news. Emma immediately called Tyrell and asked him to pick her up. She hurriedly got dressed and collected her things.

Tyrell appeared thirty minutes later.

"All set?" asked her associate.

"Yeah, I think I have everything," replied Emma as she glanced around the room.

"I got you a rental car. It's parked in your driveway. Your insurance company wants you to call them with a few more details."

"Thanks, Tyrell. You're the best!"

"I know that, girl!" he said jokingly. "You just take it easy for a while, you hear?"

"I hear," mimicked Emma.

The two friends left the hospital in good spirits. On the drive home, Emma filled him in with more details of her crash two nights earlier.

Tyrell shook his head as she recounted the harrowing ordeal. "I think someone was watching over you, girl! It's a miracle you're still here."

"That's for sure. I would like to know who that mystery man was, though."

"Yeah…seems strange he just appeared and then… disappeared," mused Tyrell. "And he didn't even give you his name?"

"Nope. He appeared, pulled me from the car, and then vanished."

"Well, that sure is one for the books!"

"It sure is," agreed Emma.

Tyrell pulled his Jeep into Emma's driveway and said, "See you tomorrow?"

"I'm going to have a hot shower, and then I'll probably come by the office in a couple of hours."

"You sure you don't even want to take the rest of the day off? You've been through a lot."

"Thank you for your concern, but I'll be fine." With that, Emma opened the Jeep's door and headed toward her house. She turned and waved as she approached her door. "See you later."

Tyrell just shook his head and smiled as he shoved his Jeep into reverse.

†††

A shower had never seemed as refreshing as this one, thought Emma as she put on fresh business clothes. She checked for her mail and then relaxed with a light lunch as she read through it.

After finishing her lunch, she packed her briefcase and headed out. Tyrell had rented her a silver mid-size sedan, which, as he said, was parked in her driveway. She paused to appreciate again how much she relied on him. She climbed into the car, pushed start, and drove away towards her office.

Maggie Barnett embraced Emma as she entered the reception area of her office. "Oh, Emma, I was so worried about you!" she cried.

"Thanks for your concern, Maggie, but I'm alright. Just a little bruised up, that's all."

"How's the rental? Is it what you wanted?"

"Its fine, Maggie. Did *you* look after it?"

Maggie nodded.

Emma continued playfully, "And all along I thought Tyrell handled it!"

The three friends chuckled, and then Emma invited Tyrell into her office. "Alright, I met with James Miesner at his office in Toronto Tuesday evening."

"How did that go?" inquired Tyrell.

"Well, I'm not sure." Emma rose from her chair carefully, wincing slightly, and began to pace. "He's a man who knows what he wants, and I believe he usually *gets* what he wants."

"Does he want us?" asked Tyrell.

"No doubt about it. He wants us." Emma paused for a few seconds as she paced. "I'm just not sure whether or not we want him."

"What do you mean?"

"Obviously this would be a very lucrative account. Mr. Miesner is very wealthy. But there seems to be something off about him."

"Something off?" questioned Tyrell.

"Yeah," said Emma as she returned to her chair. "I have no interest in involving our firm with anything that is not above board."

"What makes you think he may not be above board?"

"Just a feeling, mostly, but he seems to make a tremendous amount of money for the business he is in. He deals in real estate; high end real estate. That in itself can be very profitable, but the wealth he appears to have is astronomical. It just doesn't feel right, somehow."

"Well, you're instincts are usually very good, Emma. I would tend to think there's something there if you have that gut feeling."

"Tell you what. Let's do a deep dive into Mr. Miesner's company. I will absolutely not place this firm into something illegal. We can start laying out a plan of action today and hopefully find out what Mr. Miesner is up to."

"Sounds good, Boss. Let's get at it."

Thursday, June 11

Emma turned on her kitchen television the next morning as she sat down for her usual breakfast of cereal and fruit. She liked to remain current with local and world news and was greeted with the usual stories and videos of unrest across the globe. It was evident that the world was in more considerable disarray than ever since the Covid-19 pandemic had its three-year grip on the planet several years ago. She had never before witnessed the chaos and anarchy that was currently enveloping the world. Emma shook her head slowly as she finished her breakfast and hit 'off' on her remote. *Lord, help us,* she thought, as she rose from the table and collected her dishes.

Her cell phone buzzed. "Hey, Tyrell. What's up?"

"Hey, girl. How you feeling this morning?"

"Good. Still a little sore, but I'm fine."

"I turned up something interesting last night on our friend, Mr. Miesner."

"I'm just about to leave for the office. Meet you there in a half hour."

"Sounds good. See you in thirty."

Emma quickly dried her hair, brushed her teeth again, and was ready to head to her office.

†††

"Good morning, Maggie," said Emma cheerfully as she entered her office building. It was an unassuming building with a reception area, an office for her, one for Tyrell, and a spare which she kept ready for when she took on a partner. It was tastefully decorated with modern furniture and paintings by local artists.

Emma had done very well in the few years with her law practice, which allowed her to purchase the office building. Becoming a lawyer had not been a life-long dream of Emma's. In fact, in her younger days, practicing law was the furthest thing from her mind. It wasn't until sometime after her accident as a teenager that she suddenly felt an overwhelming compulsion to enter law school. *There must be a reason,* she had said to herself at the time.

"Good morning to you, Emma. You're looking a little more chipper today," quipped Tyrell.

"I'm feeling much better," replied Emma as she noticed her associate through the open door of his office. She smiled and motioned towards her office.

Tyrell joined her a couple of minutes later, and grabbed a spare chair and sat across from her desk.

"Okay, what have you?" asked Emma with burning anticipation.

Tyrell opened his briefcase and began to explain, "Well, I asked myself last night, why James Miesner would choose our small firm to deal with his legal issues. There are plenty of large law firms in this city with armies of lawyers who would gladly take him on as a client." He opened a folder and laid a couple of papers out on Emma's desk. "Now, if you look at his total income from the properties that he bought and sold last year, it is nowhere near the amount that is needed to sustain a company the size of his so-called Tech firm. Now, I've searched extensively for production reports from his company and I have come up empty. I tell you, his company is fraudulent."

"You thinking money laundering?"

"That would be my guess," replied Tyrell nodding his head. "He probably thinks that a small firm like us would be thrilled to have him as a client and not ask any questions. He's likely afraid that a larger firm would not want to be involved with him and possibly even expose him."

"Makes sense," said Emma as she studied the papers. "Good work, Tyrell." She reclined in her chair and pondered the situation for a moment. "His account would be very lucrative for us, but as I said, we will not deal with any client who is not entirely above board. I will let him know that we are not interested."

For the rest of the morning, Emma and Tyrell discussed other active cases in which they were involved. The two friends worked well together and were building a thriving law firm that was gaining the attention of many of their peers city-wide.

Emma glanced at her watch, "How about lunch?"

"Sorry, I told Zahra I would have lunch with her at Berringers. You're welcome to join us."

"No, no," replied Emma. "I wouldn't want to intrude. I'll be fine. I may just order something for here."

"You sure, girl?"

"I'm good, thanks. You two love birds enjoy yourselves."

Tyrell and Zahra had met a couple of years previously and had immediately fallen for each other. They were married eighteen months later, and Emma thought they made the perfect couple. Zahra emigrating from her native Nigeria to Canada with her parents five years ago. She was a strikingly beautiful woman and immediately embraced her new country, although she often mockingly threatened to return to Nigeria on some frigid January days!

"Okay then, I had better run," said Tyrell as he rose from his chair. "See you after lunch."

Emma smiled as she watched him leave, silently hoping that she could one day find a relationship such as Tyrell and Zahra had.

†††

Emma arrived home around 6 pm. She walked through her front door with the comforting idea of a hot bath and a relaxing evening at home. She kicked off her shoes, greeted her orange-colored striped cat, aptly named 'Tiger', and made her way to the kitchen. After looking through her junk mail, she discarded it and switched on her television to check the evening news.

"The streets of downtown Toronto and most major cities were clogged today with protesters," came the reporter's voice.

What are they protesting now? Emma wondered as she shook her head.

The reporter continued, "The protesters are shouting anti-Christian slogans along with anti-government ones. Calls to ban Christianity have been repeated by the protesters. Estimates have the number at around twenty thousand people today. Violence broke out as the police clashed with rioters who were vandalizing businesses. At least one police cruiser was set ablaze..."

Emma switched the television off. "Don't these people have jobs to go to?" *It seems that since the pandemic, the world has constantly been protesting something,* she thought to herself. "They want to ban Christianity?" said Emma incredulously as she looked at Tiger. The orange feline was, at the moment, more concerned with the delay of his evening meal. Emma opened her refrigerator and searched for the cat food. She scooped out a generous portion for her friend and then looked for something for herself.

As Emma dined on leftover beef stew, her thoughts drifted back to the night of her accident, more specifically, to the mystery man who rescued her from certain death. *Who was he? Where did he come from? Where did he go?* She believed that she would probably never know the answers to these questions. *If nothing else, I would like the opportunity to thank him.*

Emma was suddenly jolted from her thoughts by the shrill ringing of her phone. She glanced at the screen, smiled, and pressed 'answer'.

"Hey Tyrell, don't you ever take a break?"

"Are you watching the news?" asked Tyrell, with a note of urgency in his voice.

"I had it on a while ago, but turned it off. I'm tired of the protesters."

"Check it out. Channel 7. Those rumors we've been hearing about Christianity being put on trial to have it banned. It sounds like there might be something to it."

"You've got to be kidding!" responded Emma. "I thought they were just silly rumors."

"So did I. But I tell you, Emma, they seem to be gaining some steam. Some pretty important people seem to be warming up to the idea that Christianity is bad for the world."

"Yeah, well, hopefully, it's just the latest fad and it will soon blow over. Thanks for letting me know Tyrell. I'll have a listen and we can discuss it tomorrow. See you then." Emma hit 'end' and slowly placed her phone on her kitchen counter. She switched her television back on, and for the next fifteen minutes, was dumbfounded by what she heard and saw.

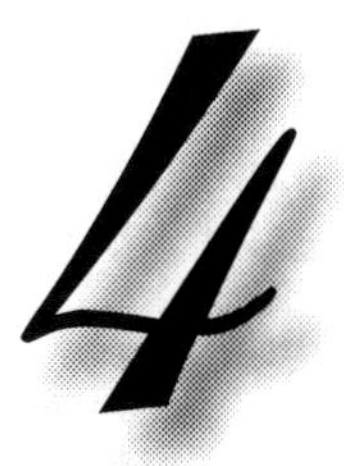

Friday, June 12

The next morning Emma arrived at her office at about 8:15. Tyrell was already at his computer, busy with a case. She tapped on his window, smiled, and waved as she strode by on her way to her office. She sat down in her pricey, ergonomic office chair and powered up her Mac as she checked her phone messages.

Tyrell knocked softly on her door frame and entered. "Did you watch any of it last night?"

"I did," answered Emma, shaking her head. "What's this old world coming to?"

"It just seems that ever since the virus, the world has been in turmoil," uttered Tyrell as he paced slowly.

"I was thinking the same thing recently. Let's just hope that this nonsense about banning Christianity blows over."

"Yeah, the world has enough problems as it is."

"Okay, we have to get started on this new case we were handed yesterday. The, uh, JM Marine Tech company."

"What's their story?" asked Tyrell as he pulled up a chair closer to Emma's desk.

"Well, they are a manufacturer of components for marine engines. They're a fair sized company doing north of twenty-five million a year." Emma continued to read her folder. "Apparently they are being accused of selling faulty components which led to a boating accident on Lake Ontario causing one fatality and several injuries. They are being sued for fifteen million. They claim that the parts were not faulty; rather that the cause was human error. JM Marine Tech seems like a good company, so I'd like to meet with them and get some more information."

"I'll get Maggie to set it up, if you would like," offered Tyrell.

"Thanks, that would be great," replied Emma as she closed the folder. "Okay, I've got a couple of other cases that we need to discuss." Emma reached for two other files on her desk and said, "Let's go to the meeting room. We'll be more comfortable there. I'll ask Maggie to join us."

The three worked through the day until late afternoon. Emma glanced at the clock on the meeting room wall; 4:55 pm.

"Why don't the two of you go home. It's Friday. Enjoy the weekend with your families. I can finish this up," offered Emma.

"You sure?" asked Tyrell. "I don't mind staying for a while."

"No, go home to your wife. I've got this. See you both Monday morning."

Tyrell and Maggie said their goodbyes and headed out the door into the hot, humid Toronto air.

Emma buried herself in her work once again for the next couple of hours.

At 7:25, feeling exhausted, she decided to call it a day. As she locked her office door, her cell phone chimed. She fumbled with her keys and her purse to get hold of the device. She glanced at the caller's name on the screen: Tyrell.

"Hey, Tyrell, what's up?"

The voice on the other end was frantic! "Slow down, Tyrell. I can't understand you," said Emma, becoming increasingly more nervous. "Say that again."

"Zahra's in the hospital!" screamed a panicked Tyrell.

"Why, what happened?" asked Emma nervously.

"She was downtown and got caught up in some rioting. She was hit in the head with a brick!"

"Oh, no!" cried Emma. "What hospital… Okay, I'll be there in thirty minutes." Emma prayed silently for Zahra as she ran to her car. As the engine roared to life, she threw it into 'drive' and squealed out of the parking lot, narrowly missing an oncoming vehicle.

Half an hour later, Emma turned into the Emergency parking lot of the Toronto Southern Hospital. She wasted no time parking and then hurried toward the Emergency entrance. As she approached the triage area, she noticed Tyrell pacing the floor nervously.

"Tyrell!" called Emma as she reached out to hug him. "What on earth happened?" She could see that her colleague's eyes were moist and puffy. "Come on, let's sit down," suggested Emma as she pointed to some nearby chairs.

Tyrell regained his composure before he began to speak. "Zahra was shopping downtown around 6 pm. She was in a shoe store and when she left the store, a riot had broken out on the street. She said it just came out of nowhere. She could see a peaceful march in the distance, and then all of a sudden it was like a war zone. People were shouting and throwing things…starting fires. She tried to escape it all, but before she could, she was hit in the head with a brick!"

"Oh, no!" cried Emma. "Poor girl!"

"She was knocked unconscious for a short time."

"Have you been able to see her?"

"Yeah, for a few minutes, then they took her down for a CT scan."

"I'm so sorry," lamented Emma. "Anything I can do for you?"

"No, thanks, Emma. I just have to wait for the doctor to give me the results of the CT scan."

"Well, I'll stay with you."

"You don't have to, Emma. I know you're busy."

"Don't be silly, Tyrell. I wouldn't think of leaving you at this time. We'll wait together. Can I get you anything?"

"No, I'm good, thanks."

The two friends waited in silence for the next forty-five minutes, each trying to comprehend what was happening.

"Mr. Lewis?" said the physician as he approached Tyrell. "I'm Doctor Rashid."

"Hi, Doctor, how is she?" asked Tyrell nervously as he and Emma stood to greet the doctor.

Doctor Rashid smiled and began, "Well Zahra's CT scan was negative. No serious brain damage. She does have a mild concussion and should take it easy for a few days, but she should be fine. She has a nasty cut on the side of her head, but we've stitched it and it should heal nicely."

"Thank you, Doctor," said a relieved Tyrell. "Can we see her?"

"Actually, she can go home, but she is to take it easy for a few days. Also it is important that you keep an eye on her for any signs of brain issues. But, I think she'll be just fine."

"Thank you, Doctor." They shook hands, and then the physician led Emma and Tyrell to the room where Zahra was recovering.

Tyrell couldn't hold back his emotions when he saw his wife with her face swollen and several stitches in her head. They hugged, Tyrell, being careful not to add to Zahra's discomfort. "I'm so glad you're okay," said Tyrell through his tears.

"I was so scared," said Zahra tearfully. "I thought I was going to die!"

"You're safe now, Zahra," said Emma comfortingly.

Zahra looked at Emma and thanked her for coming.

"Of course I would come. You and Tyrell are like family." Emma smiled warmly and asked, "Is there anything I can do for the two of you?"

"We're good, thanks," answered Tyrell. I'm just going to take Zahra home to rest."

"You just make sure you call me if you need anything over the weekend," ordered Emma. "And you go ahead and take some time off next week if you need it, Tyrell." Emma hugged Zahra gently and said her goodbyes. She left the hospital, shaking her head at the state of modern society.

Saturday, June 13

Emma awoke Saturday morning to a bright, sunny day. *Good day for a walk,* she thought. She washed, brushed her teeth, and, after putting on her grey jogging suit, left for a nearby park. The neighborhood park was a beautiful area to walk, bike, jog, or simply relax on one of the brightly-coloured benches near the impressive water fountain. Emma jogged for about twenty minutes and then decided to relax on one of the benches. She sat and watched the fountain as it spurt water in all directions. The aquatic show was so well coordinated that it reminded Emma of a symphony orchestra, with each water jet doing its part to create a spectacular array of visual excitement.

Emma reached for her metal water bottle and took a large gulp of the refreshing liquid. As she replaced the cap on her bottle, she noticed a man slowly approaching her.

"Good morning to you, miss. Mind if an old man rests here for a moment?"

Emma smiled and slid over a few inches. "Not at all!"

The man sat down with a sigh. "Thank you. My goodness, what a beautiful summer's day!" he said as he gazed at the park's splendor.

The visitor appeared to be in his early seventies, with a salt and pepper coloured beard and longish grey hair.

"Do you come to the park often?" asked the man with a friendly tone.

"Once in a while. It helps me clear my head."

"Yes, we all need to clear our heads occasionally," he replied with a chuckle.

"What about you?" asked Emma. "Do you live nearby?"

"Not far from here," was as specific as the man got. "My name is Elazar," he said as he extended his hand.

"Emma." She shook his hand.

"Good to make your acquaintance, Emma. Well, I must continue on my way." Elazar rose from the bench and smiled, "It was a pleasure to meet you." With that, he disappeared down the park bike path.

Emma watched as he ambled away, wondering who the man was. She couldn't shake the feeling that there was some familiarity in his speech and mannerisms. She pondered the meeting for a few moments, then gulped some more water, and continued with her jog.

†††

Emma returned home about forty minutes later, showered, and then enjoyed breakfast on her patio. She then called Tyrell.

"Hey, Tyrell, how is Zahra?"

"She's doing okay. Her head's still aching, but she is resting comfortably."

"Good to hear. Give her my love."

"Will do. And how are you doing?"

"I'm good, thanks," replied Emma. "I had an unusual encounter in the park this morning."

"Unusual?" queried Tyrell. "How so?"

"Well I was sitting on a park bench near the fountain this

morning, when an elderly gentleman approached and asked if he could sit down. We made small talk for a few minutes and then he went on his way."

"What's unusual about that?"

"Well, maybe nothing, but he seemed to purposely choose my bench to sit at. Also there seemed to be something familiar about him. I'm sure I don't know him, but the encounter just seemed a little strange."

"Be careful," cautioned Tyrell. "There are some peculiar people out there."

"Yeah," agreed Emma. She thought for a moment. "But maybe I'm reading too much into it."

"Maybe, but be careful, anyway," said a concerned Tyrell.

"Well, I'll let you go, Tyrell. Again, give my love to Zahra. Tell her I'm praying for her."

"Alright, thanks for calling, Emma. Bye."

Emma hit 'end' on her phone. She pondered her encounter with the man in the park briefly and then went about her day.

Monday, June 15

Monday morning was proving to be another typical July day in the city. The sun was bright, and the humidity was high. Emma arrived at her office around 7:15 am dressed fashionably in a flowery dress that she had picked up on a Hawaiian vacation the previous winter. She was usually first to arrive, then Tyrell, followed by Maggie. She wasn't sure if Tyrell would be in today or not. Emma had made it clear to him that Zahra's well-being had priority over his work.

Emma sat at her desk, powered up her Mac, and then checked her phone messages. She jotted down a few notes about each message and listed them in order of importance. She was intrigued by one particular message; a message from James Miesner.

Emma said to herself, “I thought I had made it clear to Mr. Miesner that we were unable to take him on at this time.” She did not understand why he needed her legal help anyway. Tyrell had uncovered a couple of minor lawsuits against Miesner’s corporation at present, but nothing that their present law firm couldn’t easily handle. She listened to the message again and then saved it. Emma still could not understand why someone like Miesner would be so intent on her firm representing him. Even if Emma believed Miesner to be above board, she knew that her firm did not have the resources to take on such a considerable client.

“Good morning,” came the voice through Emma’s open office door.

“What are you doing here?” said a surprised Emma. “I thought you were taking a little time off to be with Zahra.”

“She said she felt much better today and insisted I go to work,” replied Tyrell as he entered Emma’s office and sat down. “She promised she would call if anything happened.” Tyrell placed his briefcase on the floor beside his chair and asked, “So, anything new?”

“Our friend, Mr. Miesner called again.”

“He just won’t let it go, will he?” said Tyrell as he shook his head.

“He *is* determined. I’ll give him that. But, I’ll deal with him later. Right now we’ve got to prepare for the Harmond case. What have you come up with so far?”

Tyrell reached for his briefcase and removed the Albert Harmond file. Their client had been charged with assault after injuring an alleged burglar during a home invasion.

“I can’t even believe that this guy was charged. All he was doing was protecting his family,” said Tyrell.

“I agree, but he was, so we have to defend him.”

The two lawyers worked through the morning, laying out their plan for the defense of Albert Harmond.

By noon they had finalized their plan. “Let’s break for lunch,” suggested Emma. “I think we’re good to go on this case.” How about Wong’s for some Chinese?” suggested Tyrell.

“Fine with me.” The two lawyers packed up their briefcases, announced their lunch plans to Maggie, and then walked out into the brilliant sunshine.

Monday, June 29

Emma rose to deliver her closing remarks to the jury. She was dressed in a tan business suit that conveyed style and professionalism. To her left, Tyrell was watching her every move carefully. He knew that this woman would one day be a heavy hitter in the legal community. He marveled at her style and confidence and was determined to learn as much as possible from her.

"Ladies and Gentlemen of the jury, you have listened to both sides of this argument." Emma ambled toward the jury box. "You have all heard the prosecution paint a somewhat distorted picture of the events that took place that day; events that led to the altercation between my client and his accuser."

Emma Collins continued for another thirty minutes in a passionate argument that her client was well within the law to defend his home the way he did.

When she knew that she had left nothing on the table, she thanked the jury and returned to her seat, feeling drained.

"You nailed it, girl!" whispered Tyrell as he leaned in towards her.

Emma could manage only a hopeful smile.

"Thank you, Counselor," said the judge. Judge Patricia

Hainsley then directed her attention to the jury. She explained to the members what their duty was, and then had them retire to the jury room to discuss the case. Judge Hainsley then banged her gavel, adjourning the court.

"That was intense!" said Tyrell, smiling broadly. "You were amazing!"

"I just hope I was amazing enough to win."

"No problem, you got this one!"

Albert Harmond turned to Emma and asked, "What do you think."

"Well, you never know which way a jury will go. I *am* confident, though. All we can do now is pray." Emma placed her hand on his arm to reassure him. "The court will let me know when the jury has reached a verdict, and I will call you immediately."

"Thank you, Miss Collins."

Emma smiled warmly as Albert Harmond rose from his chair, joined his wife, and quietly left the courtroom.

"Come on, let's grab some lunch," suggested Tyrell.

"Sounds good, I'm starved."

Emma and Tyrell packed up their briefcases and exited the courthouse into the sweltering July noon-day sun.

†††

"I think it could go either way," stated Emma as she and Tyrell enjoyed delicious hot dogs from a local street vendor. They sat on a bench in the park adjacent to the courthouse. They wanted to stay close in case the jury was swift with their verdict.

"I think you nailed it. They'd be fools to come back with a guilty verdict," opined Tyrell as we wiped his mouth with his napkin.

"I hope you are right, my friend," as she stared across the lush park grounds.

"You can believe I'm right."

Emma's attention seemed to focus on something or someone in the distance.

"See someone you know?" queried Tyrell as he gazed in the same direction.

Emma answered hesitantly, "I'm not sure." She stared a little longer at the bearded man as he disappeared in the distance.

Emma's phone chimed. She grabbed it quickly from her purse and looked at the screen. "That was quick," she said as she pressed 'talk'. "Emma Collins,"... "Thank you." She pressed 'end', and turned Tyrell, "They're back."

"That *was* fast," replied Tyrell as he gathered up their waste and placed it in a nearby container.

Emma called her client and told him the news. She rose from the bench, took one last scan of the park, and strode off towards the courthouse.

"Are you ready?" asked Emma as she placed her hand on her client's arm.

"Yes," was the simple answer.

"Alright, let's go." The trio walked into the courtroom and took their seats. Moments later, the jury entered, followed by the judge.

The judge turned to the jury and said, "Has the jury reached a decision?"

A slender, middle-aged woman stood and replied, "We have, Your Honor."

"What say you?"

"On the charge of assault, we find the defendant not guilty. On the charge of forcible confinement, we find the defendant not guilty."

Emma, Tyrell, and Albert Harmond let out a collective sigh of relief.

"Mr. Harmond, you have been found not guilty by a jury of your peers. You are free to go. This court is adjourned." The gavel crashed down, signaling an end to the trial.

"Thank you so much, Miss Collins," said an exuberant Albert Harmond as he hugged the unsuspecting attorney. Mrs. Harmond approached the trio, smiling broadly. "Thank you so much, Miss Collins," she said as she hugged Emma. "God bless you both," she added as she hugged Tyrell.

"Glad we could be of service, Ma'am," replied Tyrell.

The greatly relieved Harmond's left the courtroom arm in arm.

Emma closed her briefcase and turned toward the rear of the courtroom to leave. She noticed a bearded man filing through the door behind the Harmond's. With a look of concern, Emma hurried to the back of the courtroom and through the door. She looked up and down the hall, but could not see the bearded man.

After catching up, Tyrell said, "What's going on?"

"That bearded man again. I thought I saw him."

"You've got that guy on your brain, girl."

Emma shook her head, "I don't know, maybe it wasn't him."

"Just some guy with a beard, that's all."

"Yeah, I guess," admitted Emma.

The two lawyers made their way out of the courthouse and back to the office.

Saturday, July 3

Emma awoke at 7 am and made her way to her park. Saturday morning had become her morning to walk or jog to enjoy the outdoors and clear her head. Today was not the typical sunny day, but rather on the gloomy side. The clouds were laden with moisture, threatening to explode with torrents of rain at any time. *Well, I guess we do need the rain,* thought Emma as she strode along the cracked sidewalk. Arriving at the park, she broke into a jog for the next twenty minutes. The morning air felt invigorating after her hectic week in the legal world. She spotted a bench a few meters ahead and decided to take a short break. She sat, pulled out her water bottle, and gulped down some of the refreshing beverage. *The rain has held off so far,* she thought as she relaxed and surveyed the park. She watched as mothers walked their babies, and children ran and bounced around on the lush grass.

"Good morning Miss Collins," came the call of a vaguely familiar voice.

Emma turned and noticed the bearded man coming towards her. He was dressed in a long trench coat with a weathered looking Aussie hat.

"Good morning to you," he repeated as he drew closer.

"Good morning," replied Emma with an uneasy smile. She still was not sure what to make of this man.

"And a lovely morning it is! It looks like rain is on the way, though. Mind if I sit?"

Emma inched over to give her visitor more room on the bench. "Be my guest."

The bearded man sat down with a sigh and gazed ahead at the various activities happening in the park.

"Could I please ask you something, Elazar?"

"Of course, Miss Collins. What is on your mind?"

"I've been noticing someone who looks a lot like you around town the last few days. The last time was in the courtroom while I was leaving. Could that have been you?"

"It could very well have been. I do get around. On occasion I stop in at the courthouse to witness our justice system in action."

"I thought you might be stalking me," said Emma.

"Gracious, no!" exclaimed Elazar. "Forgive me if I gave you that impression. But I do admit that I was fascinated with your ardent defense of Mr. Harmond. You spoke with passion and resolve, and it brought you results."

Emma smiled. "Thank you." She felt slightly more relaxed with Elazar but wanted to remain vigilant. She had come across many dangerous people in her short career and understood that she had to be cautious.

Emma asked, "Are you from around here?"

"Well, I live nearby at present, but I change residences and even countries often." He chuckled, "I suppose one could call me a citizen of the world."

"Citizen of the world? Are you a spy, or something?" asked Emma, returning his chuckle.

"Nothing quite that exiting, I am afraid. I simply, shall we say, assist people in need."

"Am I in need?" asked Emma.

"Not that I am aware of," answered Elazar. Not at the moment, anyway. The bearded man paused, and then asked, "If I may be so bold, Emma, are you a believer?"

"In God?"

"Yes, in God, and His Son."

"Yes, I am. Why do you ask?"

"I am just curious, that is all. I *thought* you were."

"How could you tell?" asked Emma.

"Oh, I can usually sense these things," replied Elazar. "Are you originally from Toronto, Miss Collins?"

"No, I'm a prairie girl. I grew up in Regina, went to university in Toronto, and then decided to stay."

"Ah, the prairies; endless skies and wheat fields as far as the eye can see," said Elazar fondly.

"Yeah, endless skies and cold winters!" mused Emma. "You've been there?"

"Why, yes indeed! I have had some marvelous experiences in the prairies. You did not wish to return?"

"I considered it, but I felt that Toronto is where I should be. My mother and step-father still live in Regina."

"Do you see them often?" asked Elazar.

"Not often enough, I'm afraid." said Emma reflectively. "We just seem to get so busy."

"I understand what you mean; our busyness can take over our lives without us even realizing it. It is something that we have to guard against. We must not let things like careers and activities rob us of our relationships with friends and loved ones."

Emma sat in silence for a moment, pondering the bearded man's insight.

"Well, I must be going, Miss Collins. Thank you, I thoroughly enjoyed our talk. Perhaps we shall meet again." Elazar rose from the bench, tipped his hat to Emma, and ambled off into the distance.

Emma sat, quietly contemplating her conversation with Elazar. He was like no one she had ever met before. She felt more comfortable with him now that they had spoken for a while. She hoped that they would meet again.

One drop, then a second. *Here comes the rain!* Emma zipped up her jacket and started for home. The drops soon became a deluge, so she began to jog. Being drenched anyway, she eventually decided to slow down to a walk and enjoy the warm, cleansing summer rain.

Monday, July 5

James Miesner sat in his luxurious office located in a small town a few minutes from the city. Although he conducted most of his business in Toronto, he preferred to live and operate his office on the outskirts. Miesner was in a foul mood today. He was livid because of Emma Collins' refusal to accept his business offer. James Miesner was a man who was used to getting what he wanted, one way or another, and Miss Collins was presenting a problem for him.

Miesner had planned to lure Emma Collins' firm into a partnership with him by offering her a lucrative case to handle for him. After gaining her confidence, his ulterior motive would then become evident. Never had he imagined that she would take the high road and refuse to deal with him.

Miesner picked up his desk phone. "Madeline, get me Emma Collins on the phone," he barked.

"Right away, Mr. Miesner," replied Madeline in a dispassionate tone.

A few moments later, Madeline buzzed her boss's phone and said, "The call went to voicemail and I left a message to call you."

Miesner muttered something derogatory about Emma and then slammed the phone down.

Madeline yanked the phone from her ear at the noise, gently replaced the receiver onto the cradle, and continued with her work. Madeline Rivera had been in James Miesner's employ for more than a dozen years. She was a skilled secretary with thick skin, which were prerequisites for remaining in James Miesner's employ. Her employer paid her well for her loyalty, and that's all that interested her.

So Miss Collins wishes to make things difficult, does she? James Miesner stared ahead while he tapped his index finger on his desk.

Miesner reached for his phone again, "Madeline, send in Charles."

"Right away, Mr. Miesner."

A few moments later, there was a light knock on Miesner's door.

"Enter," bellowed Miesner.

A man in his mid-thirties entered. Charles Egan had worked as James Miesner's assistant for just over five years. He was efficient and considered James Miesner a demanding boss, but he had learned how to handle him. Egan had gained his boss's trust and confidence early on when he successfully made some things 'happen' that prevented his boss from some serious legal action. Shortly after being hired, Charles Egan had lied to the police and planted some incriminating evidence on Miesner's behalf to frame another man for a crime that James Miesner had committed. From that moment on, James Miesner knew that Charles Egan was a vital asset for his operation.

"You wanted to see me, sir?"

"Have a seat, Charles," said Miesner, not bothering to look up from his computer screen. Thirty seconds later, he removed his reading glasses and stared for a few seconds at his associate. "We have a problem."

"What sort of problem, Mr. Miesner?"

"Emma Collins is playing hard to get. I want you to come up with some sort of idea to get her to cooperate."

"What sort of idea, boss?"

"I don't know. That's what I pay *you* for, Charles," responded Miesner flatly. "Take her on a date if you have to. Do anything to get her on our side."

"Alright, Mr. Miesner, let me work on it."

"Okay, and we don't have a lot of time, either."

Charles nodded, "If I may ask, sir, why is Emma Collins so important to you? There are plenty of capable law firms in this city to handle your business."

"I need someone who is young and naïve; someone who is eager to make a lot of money and rise to the top of her profession; someone who will do my bidding without a lot of questions."

"From the little I've heard about Miss Collins, she's pretty sharp," replied Charles.

"Well, I can handle her once we get her on board. I see a huge benefit in having her with us. She would add a lot of credibility to my business. You just take care of what I asked," said Miesner sternly.

"On it, sir," said Charles as he rose to leave.

James Miesner lifted the receiver on his phone and demanded, "Madeline, call my wife and tell her I'll be late tonight." He hung up his phone and then stared at the expensive painting on his wall for a few seconds strategizing his next move. He then shut down his computer and left his office. "I'll be out for the day," he growled as he passed by Madeline's desk.

"Very well, sir," she replied, quietly breathing a sigh of relief as he left.

†††

"How was your weekend?" asked Tyrell as he stuck his head through Emma's open office door.

Emma looked up from her computer monitor and motioned her associate to come in. "Weekend was quiet. Not much going on," she responded. "I did have another encounter, though, with my bearded friend."

"Oh, yeah?" replied Tyrell as he sat down in one of Emma's plush office chairs and placed his shoulder bag on the floor beside him. "What did he have to say this time?"

"Well, a little more than the last time. He seems to say more each time we meet. I still don't know if he has something in mind, or he is just a friendly person who wants to talk. He told me that he has lived in many different places and several countries in his lifetime. He said he is in the business of 'assisting people'."

"Assisting people? How so?" asked an intrigued Tyrell.

"He didn't say. I jokingly asked him if he was a spy. He said he wasn't."

Tyrell laughed at the notion.

"He just seems to appear out of nowhere," mused Emma. "I don't know what he's up to, if anything. Maybe he's just a friendly sort of guy."

Tyrell cautioned, "You still want to be careful. Who knows what this guy might be up to."

"Yeah, maybe I'll never see him again. Anyway, we've got a new case that we need to discuss."

The two colleagues worked through the morning researching and planning strategies for their new case.

"This is going to be a big one," commented Tyrell as he shuffled through some papers that Emma had printed for him.

"You know, if we get much busier, I'm going to have to consider hiring another associate."

"Yeah, I was thinking the same thing," agreed Tyrell.

"I'll put some feelers out, see who might be available." She looked at her watch and said, "Let's get some lunch."

Tyrell quipped, "I can't believe you still wear one of those things, girl. What are you, fifty? That's why the cell phone was invented."

Emma playfully stuck her tongue out at him and replied, "I like my watch, and no, I'm not fifty!"

The two friends laughed as they packed up their papers and then headed for their favourite restaurant.

†††

Emma and Tyrell chatted over a lunch of deli meat sandwiches and salad. They enjoyed their informal conversations away from the pressures of the office.

Tyrell asked, "So, do you ever regret leaving Regina for Toronto?"

"I sometimes miss the smaller city's slower pace, but I just feel that Toronto is where I have to be," replied Emma as she added a touch of mustard to her sandwich. "When I was recovering from my accident back when I was seventeen, a wise man told me that God had a plan for my life. I didn't think much of that at the time. I thought he was just a dreamer. Later, when a young girl that I met in the hospital died, I suspected that our short friendship might be part of this plan. After finishing university in Toronto, I thought that this city is where I belonged; it just felt right."

"God must have something big planned for you, girl," said Tyrell as he took a sip of his water. "He's layin' it out for you! You have a talent that I have never seen before in this business."

"Maybe, I don't know," replied Emma with an unsure tone in her voice.

"Yes, ma'am, something big is coming your way! I can feel it!"

Emma laughed, "You and your *feelings*..."

"Have I ever been wrong?" asked Tyrell with a smirk.

Emma responded with 'the look', causing the two of them to burst out laughing. They enjoyed the rest of their lunch, paid their bill, and then stepped outside to begin their walk back to the office.

They reached their office parking lot several minutes later and slipped through the front door, oblivious to the lone occupant in the white Ford Escape across the street. Once they had disappeared inside, the driver of the Escape started his engine and sped off.

After a busy afternoon, Emma decided that it was time to call it a day. It was 6:30, and Tyrell and Maggie had left an hour earlier. Emma was aware that she was still swamped with work, but decided that she had been at the office long enough. She packed her shoulder bag with the intent of working at home for a couple of hours in the evening. *I've got to hire someone soon,* thought Emma, while walking out of her office into the warm summer air. She powered up her new Buick Envision and headed out onto the busy street, unaware of the white Escape following a short distance behind.

Saturday, July 10

Saturday morning dawned bright and sunny in downtown Toronto. Dressed in a light grey tracksuit with pink accents, Emma left her apartment for her Saturday morning walk and jog. She felt invigorated by the light morning breeze that was causing the lush neighborhood trees to sway slightly. Within a few minutes, she arrived at her favourite park. It was just after 7 am and the park was still relatively quiet. She began to jog along the bike path as she cleared her mind of the past week's challenges and stressful moments. After a half-hour, she decided to take a break on one of the park benches. She removed the cap from her water bottle and gulped down some of the refreshing liquid. Emma sat for a few moments, just absorbing the beauty of her surroundings. She wondered if she might meet Elazar again today in the park.

"Good morning," said the voice, causing Emma to turn her head in its direction quickly. "Mind if I sit?"

The voice wasn't Elazar's.

"Uh, sure," responded Emma hesitantly. She didn't want to be paranoid, but she *did* want to be careful.

The man sat at the opposite end of the bench. "Beautiful day!"

"Uh, yes it is," replied Emma, trying to mask her uncertainty.

"My name is Charles," said the visitor as he stretched out his hand.

"Emma."

"Do you come here often, Emma?"

"Occasionally," she answered, unsure of how much information she should share with this person.

"I'm new to the area, so I'm still trying to familiarize myself with all it has to offer," said Charles with a smile.

"It is a wonderful park," offered Emma, as she gazed across the lush, opulent greenery.

"So, Emma, have you lived here long?"

"You mean in Toronto?"

"Yeah."

"I went to university here, and then decided to stay. I'm originally from Regina."

"What do you do, Emma?" asked Charles.

Why so many questions? What does this guy want? Maybe he's just the friendly, out-going type. A barrage of questions about this man's intentions filled Emma's mind. She decided to be very careful what information that she shared with him. "I'm a lawyer."

"A lawyer! You don't look the type."

"Looks can be deceiving," replied Emma, deciding that she had offered enough information about herself to this stranger. "Well, I've got to continue on my jog," She took another gulp of water. "Nice meeting you, Charles." Emma stood, smiled, and went on her way. Charles watched her as she jogged out of sight.

Charles Egan contemplated his next move for a few moments and then headed off toward his white Escape.

Emma arrived home about thirty minutes later, took a cool shower, and then sat down for a breakfast of cereal, fruit, and coffee. She contemplated her meeting in the park with Charles, still wondering whether his motives were innocent or not. She decided to put him out of her mind for now and get on with her day. Emma picked up her phone, searched her contacts, and pressed her mother's name.

"Hi, Mom, how are you?"

"We're both well, honey, and how are you feeling?"

"I'm fine. The soreness is gone. I feel pretty good; almost back to normal."

"Ben and I were thinking of coming out to Toronto for a visit," said Heather.

"Sounds great!" replied Emma.

"We were thinking next month for a few days."

"That would be wonderful. I'll arrange to have a couple of free days while you're here."

Emma and her mother talked for the next twenty minutes, planning Heather and Ben's visit to Toronto.

"Okay, I'll call you next week, bye, Mom." Emma pressed 'end' and placed her phone back on her kitchen counter. She was excited about seeing her mother and Ben but had no idea how she could take any time off. Emma began to straighten up her kitchen when her phone chimed.

"Hey Tyrell, what's up?"

"Hey Emma, Zahra wants to know if you'd like to join us at our church tomorrow. Maybe we can go for lunch afterwards."

"Sure, I'd love to. What time is it, again?"

"Meet you there about 9:45."

"Sounds good; see you there," confirmed Emma. Again, she pressed 'end' and put her phone down on the counter. Emma spent the rest of the day on her laptop, working.

Sunday, July 11

Emma pulled into Grace Church parking lot at precisely 9:45 the next morning. Zahra and Tyrell were waiting by the door and greeted their friend with warm hugs.

“Glad you could make it, Emma,” said Zahra as she smiled and held both of Emma’s hands.

“Wouldn’t miss one of your great services!”

“Come on, let’s go in so we can get a good seat,” suggested Tyrell.

For the next ninety minutes, Emma and her friends enjoyed the powerful and moving service. The church was packed, creating an energetic and dynamic atmosphere. When the service ended, the trio slowly headed for the exit, greeting a steady stream of worshippers as they made their way out. As they stepped out into the brilliant sunshine, Emma was surprised to hear someone behind her call her name. She turned and was taken aback by who was behind her.

“Charles?” said Emma in an uncertain tone.

“We meet again! How are you?” said Charles with a broad smile.

“I’m surprised to see you here. Is this your church?” asked Emma, not quite sure what to make of this chance meeting.

“No, I don’t usually go to church, but I thought I would give it a try today,”

Emma smiled nervously and then introduced her friends. “Tyrell and Zahra, this is Charles Egan. I met him in the park yesterday.”

They shook hands and greeted each other warmly. “Good to meet the two of you,” said Charles. “Great church you have here,” he added.

“Thanks, we enjoy it,” replied Tyrell.

They all walked together to the parking lot.

“I’m over here,” said Charles, pointing to a white Ford Escape. “Nice to meet you both. Hope to see you again. Bye, Emma.”

Emma just nodded as Charles strode off towards his SUV.

“So, you met him in the park,” commented Tyrell.

“Yeah, yesterday. He showed up and asked if he could sit on the bench with me.”

"What did he have to say?" inquired Zahra.

"Nothing much, just small talk; that's all."

"Does it seemed strange to you that this guy meets you in the park, and then shows up at the same church you are visiting the next day?" asked Tyrell.

"Could be a coincidence," offered Zahra.

"Sounds a little off to me," countered Tyrell as he watched the white Escape disappear down the street. "Be careful, girl. This guy could be up to something."

"Thank you for your concern, Tyrell, but I will be fine."

"How about joining us for lunch, Emma," suggested Zahra. "We're going to Berringer's."

"Love to."

"Great, meet you there," said Zahra.

Emma walked to her vehicle and powered it up, turning the air conditioning on high. She slowly weaved her way through the crowded lot and entered the street on her way to the restaurant. As she drove, she overlooked the inconspicuous white Ford Escape that sat idling on the side of the street.

Monday, July 12

"Collins and Associate Law Office; how may I help you?" said Maggie Barnett as she clicked on her headset.

"I'd like to speak to Emma Collins," said the man's voice on the line.

"Miss Collins is out of the office at the moment. Could I ask who's calling, please?"

"Just a friend," was the strangely vague answer. "When will she be in?" asked the man.

"I'm not sure. Sir, if you give me your name and number I can have her call you when she gets back to the office."

"No need; I'll call back later," was the man's reply. With that, he abruptly hung up.

Maggie stared quizzically at the phone for a moment, shook her head, and then clicked off her headset. She wrote down a quick note regarding the call and then continued on with her work.

"Good morning, Maggie," said Emma as she entered the office building. "Any calls?"

"I left a few messages on your desk. I also had a strange call about an hour ago."

"Strange? How so?" asked Emma.

"Well, a man called for you. Unknown number came up. He wouldn't give me his name or number. He said he was a friend and that he would call back. Then he just hung up."

"That *is* strange," agreed Emma as she thought for a moment. "We'll see if he calls back." Emma waved at Tyrell through his glass office wall and then headed to her office and powered up her Mac.

Tyrell joined his boss a few minutes later. "Hey, how are you?" he asked.

"I'm fine, and how are you doing?"

"I'm good. What's this about a strange phone call?"

"Oh, Maggie got a call, asking for me. The caller wouldn't leave his name or number. Said he will call back. It's probably nothing," said Emma, as she tried hard to believe her words.

"I hope you're right," said Tyrell. "Changing the subject; have you been following the news the last couple of days?"

"Somewhat," responded Emma. "Why, what's going on?"

"The protesters again. It's happening all around the world. Protesters all over the place."

"What are they upset about now?" asked Emma.

"It seems that Christianity has really become the target. There is a growing push to have it completely banned."

"From where?"

"Everywhere. Turn on the news and check it out."

Emma turned on the television set in her office and switched it to a twenty-four hour news channel. Tyrell and Emma watched in disbelief for the next twenty minutes, shaking their heads periodically. The reporter was covering a massive demonstration in London, calling for the end of Christianity. She reported that similar demonstrations were being held all over. She claimed that governments throughout the world were looking for ways to appease the protesters.

"Why has Christianity become such a target?" Emma wondered out loud.

Tyrell said, "It seems that ever since the world was shaken for three years by COVID 19, there has been growing unrest. For some reason Christianity has stirred up the ire of a lot of people; I just don't know why. I've got to tell you, though, it kind of makes me nervous."

"Yeah, I hear you," agreed Emma.

They watched for another few minutes and then turned the television off and went back to work.

"By the way, I've placed an online ad for another lawyer," said Emma. "Our caseload has gotten too much for the two of us to handle."

"Sounds good," said Tyrell.

"Yeah, I hope to have someone within the next couple of weeks. Also, I'd appreciate it if you could sit in on the interviews. I'd like to have your take on each one."

"Sure thing, Emma. I'd be happy to."

"Good. I'll probably schedule some by the end of the week."

Emma's desk phone buzzed. "Yes, Maggie?"

"The caller from earlier is on the line, Emma. Do you wish to take it?" asked Maggie.

"Did he say who he was?"

"He wouldn't say."

"Okay, thanks, Maggie, I'll take it." She pressed Line 1. "Emma Collins; How can I help you?"

"Hello, Miss Collins, how are you?"

Emma hesitated and then said, "I'm fine. Do I know you?"

"Charles Egan," said the caller.

There was silence on the line for a few moments. Emma had not expected this. "Uh, hello, Charles. What can I do for you?"

"Just thought I'd give you a call to see how you were."

Again, there was silence on the line. "As I said, I'm fine. Is there anything else you need?"

"Actually, there is. I was wondering if you would have dinner with me tomorrow night."

Emma was dumbfounded! *Who is this guy? What does he want?* Emma collected her thoughts and then replied, "I've got a big week in front of me. I'm very busy all this week, I'm afraid."

"That's too bad. How about next week?"

"Uh, I'm really not sure, Charles. Things are getting pretty hectic around here."

"How about I call you next week?" asked Charles.

Silence again for a moment. "Uh, yeah, I suppose. No promises, though."

"Fair enough. I'll call you next week. Goodbye."

Emma just stared at the receiver for a moment and then gently placed it back on its cradle.

"What was that all about?" asked Tyrell.

"He asked me for a date! I just met the guy."

"Be careful. Like I said, something seems off with this guy."

"Well, I don't know about that, but, I have way too much work to do right now to be thinking about dating," Emma said dismissively. She reached for a folder on her desk and said, "Okay let's finish discussing strategy for the Mitchell case."

An uneasy feeling crept into Emma's consciousness.

Saturday, July 17

Emma set out for her run at about 8 am on Saturday. The July sun beat down on the still damp sidewalk. An overnight rain shower had cleared the humidity, leaving the air fresh, and Emma feeling invigorated. She had slept until 7:30, which was late for her. The past week was hectic for her firm, and she felt exhausted. She hoped a run would help clear her mind of some of the stress of running her law firm.

Emma made her way to her favourite park and turned onto the bike path, picking up her speed. The warm summer breeze gently caressed her face as she navigated the winding path. Her brown hair, tied into a pony tail, waved as she ran. Emma Collins felt alive when running. It allowed her to momentarily shed her cares and feel totally free.

After about thirty minutes, she stopped by a park bench for a drink and a short rest. She sat down and uncapped her bottle as she gazed out at the scenic park. She was never tired of its beauty.

"Miss Collins," called the nearby voice.

Emma turned and was surprised to see Elazar approaching her. *How does he keep finding me?* "Elazar, what are you doing here?" Emma wasn't sure whether to be happy to see him or nervous about him showing up again.

"Well, it was such a magnificent morning, that I thought I would take a leisurely walk in the park. To be perfectly honest with you though, I did hope that I would see you here." Elazar paused for a moment. "If you don't mind, I would like to continue our conversation from the last time we met."

Emma was beginning to trust this man, so she invited him to sit.

"Fabulous morning, is it not?" said Elazar as he sat down on the hard bench.

"Yes it is." Emma was starting to feel a little more comfortable with the bearded man.

"So, Miss Collins, how was your week?" asked Elazar as he removed his Aussie hat and wiped his brow.

"Please, Elazar, it's Emma."

Elazar chuckled, "Very well, Emma; how was your week?"

"Long and stressful, like usual."

"That *is* a shame, because I understand that you are a gifted attorney."

"Where did you hear that?"

"Oh, here and there. You are building quite a reputation in the legal community. From what I understand it is a reputation of fairness and tenacity. You should be proud."

"Well, I have a terrific associate who is invaluable to me. He'll be partner one day. Our case load is increasing at a tremendous pace, so I hired another associate yesterday to take some of the pressure off of Tyrell and myself. I'll probably have to hire someone else before long."

"Well, that sounds exciting; good for you," said Elazar with a smile. The bearded man thought for a moment; "I'm not a prophet, Emma, but I believe something big is coming your way. I don't know what it might be, but I do believe it will be something of significance."

Emma looked at the Elazar quizzically, wondering what on earth he was talking about.

"You told me that you were a believer, Emma, so you know where your trust must lie. That trust in God will see you through these difficult times. Times when you feel overwhelmed…times when you think you cannot continue. He will see you through."

Emma nodded her head as she absorbed the wisdom from Elazar. She had heard these words before, but coming from this man, they seemed to resonate in her mind. She still did not understand his intentions, but more and more felt drawn to him. Any fear of this man had vanished and had been replaced with peace of mind.

"So, Emma, what are your aspirations for the future?" asked Elazar.

Emma thought for a moment. "Well, my main focus in business is to help people with their legal issues. I try to be selective in who I represent. Occasionally, I will refuse someone who I think is trying to skirt the law; trying to use my firm for gain in an underhanded way. This sometimes comes at a financial cost to me, but I believe that is the way God would have me conduct my business."

"That is admirable," said Elazar.

"A long time ago, when I lived in Regina, someone told me that God had a plan for my life." Emma paused for a moment, "I don't know; maybe my law practice is part of that plan."

"I suspect that it is, and I am almost certain that the entire *plan* has not yet been revealed. You must keep your eyes on God and let Him guide your steps. Tell me, Emma, what circumstances brought you to believing that He had a plan for your life?"

"Well, when I was seventeen I was hit by a car and was hospitalized for a while. I was already in a bad state emotionally and the accident made things worse." Emma sniffed and wiped a tear from her eye. "Sorry, I still get a little teary-eyed when I tell this story."

"Quite alright, my dear," said Elazar with a warm smile. "Please continue."

"Well, I met a ten year old girl in the hospital who was dying of a rare disease. We eventually became friends and her faith amazed me. I realized that this girl's problems were so much worse than mine, but she had such a positive outlook on things. She told me that her faith gave her that positive attitude. I was ashamed of my behavior and asked God for His forgiveness. That's about it. Here I am."

"That is a fascinating story, Emma. May I say that this young girl's death, as horrible as it was, served as part of the plan that will eventually benefit untold numbers of people?" said Elazar. Many people do not realize the plan that God has for their lives, until the plan comes to fruition. It is sometimes difficult to recognize His work until it is complete."

Emma slowly nodded her head as she contemplated Elazar's words. The bearded man had a way about him that she had never witnessed before. She found herself hanging on every word that he uttered. He exuded an air of confidence while his insight into her life was uncanny. Emma was beginning to believe that she could trust Elazar with her innermost thoughts.

"I would not be surprised," continued Elazar, "if you notice more and more of the plan being revealed as time goes by. I believe that you are in for a most exciting future, Emma! Just remember where to keep your focus."

Elazar placed his old weathered hat back on his head and said, "Well, Emma, it has been a pleasure speaking with you once again, but I must bid you farewell for now." He rose from the bench, smiled, tipped his hat toward Emma, and sauntered off down the path.

Emma watched as he disappeared in the distance. She sat for several more minutes considering Elazar's words. A gentle breeze had begun to blow, creating a refreshing coolness in the warm summer air. Emma felt invigorated. She rose from the bench energized and resumed her run at a quickened pace.

As she entered her front door, she was met by a surly feline who was less than pleased at being made to wait longer than usual for his breakfast. Tiger was accustomed to eating no later than 7:30 am, and it was now almost 8:45. He made no secret of his displeasure.

"Sorry, Tiger," said Emma in feigned concern. She opened a can of his favourite tuna and chuckled as she watched him devour it. She switched on her kitchen television and went about preparing breakfast. Emma shook her head as she listened to the news story that caught her attention. Demonstrations were still happening in many parts of the world. She felt saddened that Christianity had become such a target of unrest. Emma switched off the television and then sat down for her Saturday morning breakfast.

August 4

Emma sat at her computer in her office, working through her immense caseload. She paused for a moment and gazed out of her window at the bleak autumn sky. The grey clouds and chilly temperature confirmed that another winter was on its way.

The buzz of her desk phone jolted her from her momentary daydream. She reached for her phone. "Yes, Maggie?"

"You won't believe this, but there is a Reverend Einer Nordstrom from the World Council of Churches. He wishes to speak to you."

"What? Are you sure?" asked Emma incredulously.

"That is what he said. Are you in?"

"Of course!" exclaimed Emma. "Just give me thirty seconds and then put him on." Emma mouthed the word "wow" and then quickly composed herself.

"Reverend Nordstrom; to what do I owe the honour?" said Emma trying hard not to sound over-excited.

"The honour is all mine, Miss Collins. I have been looking forward to speaking with you. If I may, I would very much appreciate a short meeting with you in the near future, if your schedule would allow."

"Absolutely, Reverend! When would you like to meet?"

"Next week would be fine, if you are available."

"Could I be so bold as to ask what this meeting concerns?"

"The offer of a once in a lifetime opportunity, Miss Collins. That is about all I am at liberty to say until we meet face to face."

Emma grabbed for her appointment book. "Would next Monday, the 11th suit you? Say 10 am?"

"That would be outstanding! Monday, the 11th it is. I shall see you then, Miss Collins and thank you so much. Good day to you."

"Emma cradled her phone receiver and stared straight ahead for several moments. *What on earth could the World Council of Churches want with me?* Emma reached for her phone again. "Yes, Maggie, could you come in for a minute and bring Tyrell and Jeff? Thank you."

"What's up, Boss?" said Tyrell as the three entered Emma's office.

"Have a seat. I just had a call from Reverend Nordstrom from the World Council of Churches."

"What? You're kidding, right?" said Tyrell.

"He wants to meet with me next week."

Maggie asked, "Did he say why?"

"He said he will explain when we meet. I have no idea what it is about. He just told me that it concerns a once in a life time opportunity. He wouldn't offer any more details until we meet next week. Oh, yes, Maggie, mark me down for 10 am next Monday. Until then, I would appreciate nothing being said about this."

They nodded in agreement as Maggie and Jeff rose from their chairs and left Emma's office. Tyrell stayed behind for a few minutes.

"This is wild! What do you make of it?" asked Tyrell.

"I have no idea. We'll have to wait until next week to find out. So, until then, we have more than enough to keep us busy."

"Okay. I guess we'll just have to wait and see."

"Yes, that's all we can do. It's probably not a big deal anyway."

"Well, I don't know. It must be big enough for an important guy like that to come calling."

"Yes, well, we'll see. Uh, have you done any more on the Chambers file?"

"Yeah, in my office. I'll go and grab it." Tyrell headed back to his office to collect the file.

†††

Emma arrived home around 6 pm that evening. She grabbed the handful of mail from her mailbox and walked through her door, wondering what mood Tiger would be in this evening. Walking into her kitchen, she noticed something in her mail which seemed odd. She placed the mail on her counter and looked at the odd piece of paper. It appeared to be a handwritten note. She opened it and furrowed her brow as she read the brief anonymous message. *Whatever it is…don't get involved!*

Emma stood there motionless. "What?" she said aloud. "What's that all about? Probably just some crank." She stared at the ominous note for a few seconds, feeling somewhat unnerved. She tossed it onto the kitchen counter and went about her tasks of feeding a disgruntled Tiger and preparing dinner for herself as she struggled to get the note out of her mind.

Emma picked at her dinner of warmed-up leftover casserole from the day before. She couldn't shake the uneasy feeling she had after reading the note. *Whatever it is…don't get involved!* "What does that even mean?" she asked aloud. Reaching for her phone, she pressed Tyrell's number.

"Hi, Tyrell, so sorry to bother you at home, but I had to call someone."

"What's up, girl?" said Tyrell in an uneasy tone.

"I had the strangest note left in my mail box. It says *Whatever it is…don't get involved!* No name on it., of course."

"That *is* weird."

"Yeah, it's probably nothing, but it makes me a little edgy."

"Maybe you should call the cops."

"I don't know…it's not much to go on. I think I'll keep it anyway, just in case."

"Good idea. You never know what deranged people might be out there. You okay by yourself?"

"Yeah, thanks. It's probably nothing. I'm sorry I called."

"I'm glad you did. I'm here if you need me."

"Thanks, Tyrell. See you tomorrow." Emma pressed 'end' and gently placed her phone on the counter. She slipped the curious note into a plastic sandwich bag for safekeeping on the chance that the police became involved at a later time. Emma then sat, quietly pondering the disquieting message.

Monday, August 11

Emma arrived at her office before 7 am on Monday. She hadn't slept much the night before, tossing and turning as she tried to imagine what Reverend Nordstrom could want with her. As much as she told herself not to fret about it, she could not relax as her mind envisioned a plethora of possibilities.

She made a pot of coffee and then powered up her Mac, hoping to get some work done before the arrival of Reverend Nordstrom.

Promptly at 9:58, Emma's desk phone buzzed. She collected her thoughts for a moment and then lifted the receiver.

"Yes, Maggie?" she said, clearing her throat nervously.

"Reverend Nordstrom is here."

"Thank you, send him in, please."

Emma rose from her chair, took a deep breath, and walked toward her door. She opened it and reached out her hand.

"Reverend Nordstrom, wonderful to see you!" said Emma brightly, trying to mask her nervousness.

The reverend smiled broadly and shook Emma's hand gently. "I thank you, Miss Collins for taking time out of your busy schedule to accommodate me."

"Please sit, Reverend," said Emma as she offered him a chair. "Could I offer you some coffee?"

"That would be marvelous, Miss Collins. Just a little cream, please."

Emma poured two cups of steaming coffee, added some cream to each, and handed one to her guest. She returned to her seat behind her desk and picked up her phone. "Yes, Maggie, could you hold my calls please?...Thank you." She hung up her phone and turned her attention to Reverend Nordstrom. "So, Reverend Nordstrom, how can I help you?"

Reverend Nordstrom took a sip of his coffee and said, "Goodness! That is fine coffee."

"Thank you. It is a special Colombian blend that a local shop prepares for me," replied Emma proudly. "Glad you like it."

Her guest took another sip of the brew. "Yes, excellent coffee." He placed his cup on the desk and looked earnestly at Emma. "Miss Collins, you must be wondering what on earth the World Council of Churches requires from you."

"Well, it has been occupying my mind, I must admit."

"I'll get right to the point, then. You must be aware of the growing unrest throughout much of the world in recent months. Unrest that has led to calls for the banning of the Christian religion?"

"I am aware of the calls to ban Christianity, but I believed it to be all talk and that it would wane eventually."

"That is what the Council believed originally, but the calls are growing stronger by the day." Reverend Nordstrom paused for a moment and then continued. "It has evolved into something more than an angry mob venting. The movement has organized and has petitioned the World Court to ban Christianity outright."

"Can they do that?" asked Emma incredulously.

"Well, they are certainly trying, and sadly, the Court is taking them seriously."

Emma thought for a moment. "Who is behind the effort? Who is bankrolling the movement?"

"We are not entirely sure, but we have our suspicions. The Council is not sure if governments are involved or if the movement is financed privately. We are still investigating."

"Why on earth would they want to ban Christianity? What about all the other religions?" asked Emma.

"Well, Miss Collins, as we both know, Christianity is the one *true* religion in this world, and many religions and cultures consider it a threat to their existence. We actually believe that the petition is spiritually motivated."

Emma leaned back in her chair to absorb what she was hearing. After a few moments of contemplation, she asked, "And how do I fit into this, Reverend?"

"Well, Miss Collins that is why I am here today. The World Council has been watching you recently and the members are genuinely impressed."

"You've been watching me, as in spying?" asked Emma as she furrowed her brow.

"My goodness, no!" said the reverend with a chuckle. "We have simply been following your cases for some time, knowing that the day is coming when we will need special council for our case."

"And what case would that be," asked Emma, tilting her head slightly.

Reverend Nordstrom took on a somber tone. "Miss Collins, Christianity is under attack at this time. We are facing a foe who is relentless, a foe who would have us wiped from existence. We do have God on our side, so I am confident in victory, but nonetheless, we will have to fight and fight hard. Several nations have petitioned the World Court on this matter. Therefore we must mount a robust defense."

Emma sat motionless as Reverend Nordstrom spoke. His tone conveyed a message of urgency, as did his words. "So, where do I factor into this fight, Reverend?"

Reverend Nordstrom leaned back in his chair as he considered his next words. "As I said earlier, Miss Collins, we have noted your progress as a skilled attorney. The Council feels confident enough to ask you if you would be interested in representing the side of Christianity in the upcoming court case."

Emma was taken aback! "Me? There must be many more experienced lawyers than I that you could choose."

"There are, Miss Collins, but none with the faith and passion that you have. As I said, we have watched how you handle your cases and we know that you are a woman of integrity. We have not arrived at this decision quickly. Much prayer, thought and debate have gone into it. We are convinced that you are the person for us. You will, of course have any resources necessary at you disposal. The case will be heard by the International Court of Justice in The Hague, Netherlands. Of course, all of your expenses will be covered plus you will receive a handsome salary. You can use your own staff and also have access to other staff as needed."

Emma was dumbfounded. "I don't know what to say! As I said, surely there must be many more qualified lawyers than myself."

"We have looked at many others, Miss Collins, and you were the unanimous choice."

"Reverend Nordstrom, I was under the impression that the World Court was used only to settle disputes between nations."

"Normally that is the case, but with mounting pressure from so many nations they have decided to rule on this case."

"Would the decision be binding?" asked Emma.

"I believe that it would be. *That* is our challenge. It would drive Christians underground all over the world."

"How could such a ruling be enforced?"

Reverend Nordstrom motioned to Emma's television in the corner of her office. "Those crowds that you see with their anti-Christian slogans are driving this issue. They are growing exponentially in numbers and are influencing many governments throughout the world." Nordstrom thought for a moment. "As unfathomable as this idea sounds, I'm afraid it is the reality in which we live,"

"When would this trial begin?"

"Early in the new year," replied the reverend as he began to believe Emma was warming to the idea.

"The problem I have is that I have several cases on the go at the present time. If I were to accept you offer, a tremendous amount of research would have to be done."

I fully understand, Miss Collins. I realize that this is asking a great deal of you, but the ramifications of losing this court battle would be catastrophic. The Council will fully reimburse you for any monetary loss and pay you and your staff a considerable salary.

Emma stared down at her desk for a few moments. "Could I have some time to think about it and talk it over with my staff?"

"Absolutely, but we will need an answer by week's end."

"Of course," said Emma as she slowly nodded her head, still feeling overwhelmed.

"And I must caution you, Miss Collins, that should you accept this challenge, there are forces that may come against you. I do not mean to frighten you, but you must be aware of the gravity of this situation."

Emma thought back to the note that she found in her mailbox. A slight chill ran down her spine. "I understand."

"Very well, then, thank you so much for your time, Miss Collins," said Reverend Nordstrom as he rose from his chair and picked up his briefcase. "I will contact you in the next few days."

Emma rose and shook the reverend's hand and walked him to the door. They exchanged 'good-byes,' and then Emma closed the door slowly behind him. She stood with her hand on the door handle for a few seconds and then slowly walked back to her desk. She picked up her phone and buzzed Maggie. "Maggie, could you ask Tyrell to come in for a moment? Thanks."

"What's up," said Tyrell as he entered.

"Have a seat. I've got lots to tell you."

"You sound serious," said Tyrell, noticing the tone of his boss's voice.

Emma proceeded to relay an abbreviated version of her meeting with Reverend Nordstrom.

"So, that's it in a nutshell," said Emma.

"Wow!" was all that Tyrell could muster. "What are you going to do?"

"That's the question I hope you can help me answer."

"Well, from where I sit it looks like an incredible opportunity. A case like this doesn't come around very often."

"Yeah you're right about that," mused Emma. "I'm just not sure that we would be able to handle such a prodigious case with our small firm."

"I'm sure that the Council of Churches took that into consideration before they approached you. They must trust your abilities."

"Yeah, I guess so," agreed Emma half-heartedly. "What do you think, Tyrell? Be honest with me because if we accept this case there is no turning back. We'd be in it for the long haul."

"Well, girl, you're the boss, but I think we should totally go for it. Not only would we serve God through this case, but just think what a win would do for the firm!"

"You're right about that," said Emma as she rose from her chair and made her way to her large office window. She stood and stared silently out at the busy Toronto street. For several minutes she watched the traffic and pedestrians hurry by, going about their daily lives. "So many people," she said softly, "with so little hope. The outcome of this trial will affect countless people." She stared for several more seconds. "Tyrell, let's do it!"

"Yes! Now you're talking!" exclaimed Tyrell as he clapped his hands together.

Emma returned to her desk. "Okay, this case will entail a huge amount of research."

"What about our current cases?" asked Tyrell.

"They're going have to be cleared up quickly because it will be necessary to put all our efforts into this new case. I'll fill the others in on what's happening, and then we can start planning. I'm afraid Jeff is going to have to bare a lot of the load of current cases." Emma buzzed her secretary, "Maggie, would you and Jeff come in, please? Thanks."

August 15

The warm morning sun was promising another scorching August day. Emma arrived at her office at 7 am, eager to tackle another day of preparation for her upcoming extraordinary case. She clumsily managed to unlock her door as she juggled her briefcase, an armload of books, and her large cup of coffee. Finally, reaching her desk with her coffee still in the cup, Emma let out a "whew!" as she sat down and powered up her Mac. Taking a sip of her hot beverage, she pressed 'voicemail' on her phone.

Hello, Emma. Charles Egan here. Just wondering if I could interest you in dinner tonight? Give me a call. Bye.

Emma sighed as she clicked off the voicemail button. "I guess he's not going to leave me alone! I suppose one dinner wouldn't hurt." She picked up her phone and dialed Charles' number. "Hello, Charles, Emma Collins... Yeah, how about tonight?...Alright, I'll meet you there. Bye." Emma hung up the phone and stared straight ahead for a moment. *I hope I won't regret this.*

"Knock, knock, anybody home?" said Tyrell as he peered into his boss's office.

"Come on in," said Emma as she waved to him. "How's the research going?"

"It's coming along. That world court is a complex machine, but I think I'm starting to understand how it works."

"Good. Keep at it," replied Emma as she turned to the computer screen. "Guess who I'm going to dinner with tonight."

Tyrell stared at her with a questioning look.

"Charles Egan."

"What?" asked Tyrell incredulously, "Charles Egan?"

"Well, he kept calling, so I thought I might as well see what he's up to."

"I think I know what he's up to. It seems pretty obvious to me," said Tyrell in a cautioning tone. "I wouldn't trust that guy."

"I don't think *that* is what he's after. I think it has something to do with the firm. I'm just not sure what."

"Just be careful, okay?"

"Yes, Mother," chuckled Emma.

"I'm serious, girl. You don't know what this guy is up to," replied Tyrell soberly. "Call me if you need any help."

"I will." Emma tilted her head slightly and smiled. "Now, get back to work!" she chided playfully.

Tyrell shook his head, feigning anger, and returned to his office.

†††

Emma glanced at her watch and decided it was time to head home and get ready for her 'dinner date'. She powered down her Mac, stuffed some papers into her briefcase, and headed for the door. It was 6:15 pm, and she was meeting Charles at 7:30. It would leave her just enough time to drive home, have a shower and get to the restaurant.

Charles was already seated at the upscale restaurant when Emma arrived. She looked elegant in her pale blue dress as the maitre d' escorted her to the table where Charles was perusing the extensive menu. He rose and greeted Emma as she arrived, "I'm so glad you could make it."

"Well, you are quite persistent," said Emma as she sat down on the plush velour chair.

"I took the liberty of ordering a bottle of wine. I hope you like it," said Charles.

"I'm sorry, Charles, I don't drink," replied Emma.

"That's quite alright. What would you like?"

Emma looked at the waiter, "Sparkling water would be fine, thank you."

"Very well, Ma'am," said the waiter as he smiled and left.

"You look amazing," offered Charles as he took a sip of his wine.

"Thank you." Emma forced an awkward smile, still feeling uncomfortable.

The waiter returned with Emma's water and took their order.

"So, how is your law firm doing?" inquired Charles.

"We're holding our own," replied Emma. "I recently took on another associate. Things are going quite well at the moment."

"So, what cases are you working on right now?"

Emma was beginning to feel uneasy with Charles' questions. "Oh, we have several things on the go at the moment," she replied, not wanting to offer too many details until she knew what he was after. "What about your business?"

"Busy, busy, busy. Always lots to do," answered Charles vaguely.

Their waiter arrived with their salads and placed them on the table.

"Do you mind if I say grace?" queried Emma.

"Uh, no. Of course not," replied Charles.

The two diners made small talk for the next quarter-hour leading Emma to believe that it could prove to be an enjoyable evening out.

"So, what big case is Collins and Associates working on now?" asked Charles as he took another sip of wine.

Emma considered it a rather odd question, so she chose to be coy with her response. "Well, we're working on different things. Some are still pending so I am not at liberty to discuss them."

"You must have some case that you can talk about!"

"I would rather not discuss my ongoing *or* future cases. It would be very unprofessional of me," retorted Emma. She was beginning to feel very uneasy with the direction of the conversation. It was becoming clear to her that Charles was up to something; just what, she had no idea. *He's definitely fishing for information on something! But, what?* Emma's suspicions were mounting.

They finished their dinner in awkward silence.

"Would you care for dessert, ma'am?" asked the waiter.

"Just some coffee, please," replied Emma.

"Make that two," added Charles.

When their coffee was finished, Emma said, "Well, I have a big day tomorrow, so I think I'll call it an evening. Thank you for the dinner, Charles; it was lovely."

Charles paid the cheque and walked Emma to her car. As they reached her vehicle, he took hold of her hand. She quickly pulled it away. "I've had a very long day, Charles."

"Of course," replied Charles, clearly disappointed.

"Good night and thank you again for the dinner." Emma slipped into her SUV, powered up the engine, and eased the vehicle out of the parking spot onto the street.

Charles stared menacingly at the Buick until it disappeared. "Next time!" he growled as he turned and walked towards his car.

August 16

Emma entered her office building the following morning and noticed Tyrell already at his computer. She knocked on his open door and walked in.

"Hey, girl," said Tyrell with a huge grin. "How was the date?"

"It wasn't a date!" replied Emma tersely as she sat down.

Tyrell shrugged sheepishly, "Sorry. Went that bad, did it?"

Emma shook her head. "I don't know what he was after, but he wanted something."

"Pretty obvious to me," offered Tyrell.

"Well, he did grab hold of my hand, but he wanted something more than that. It seemed like he was fishing for information. He kept asking me what cases we were working on."

"Do you think he might be wondering about the World Court case we have coming up?"

"I don't know how he would even be aware of it, or why he would care, for that matter," Emma said, shaking her head.

"Well, he does work for James Miesner and he is a pretty connected guy. We have no idea what Miesner might know."

Tyrell walked over and closed his door. In a hushed tone, he said, "You don't think we have a problem with Jeff, do you?"

"I don't think so. I vetted him quite extensively before hiring him, so I'm sure he isn't a problem. I trust him completely," answered Emma emphatically. "As you said, James Miesner has eyes and ears all over, so it's pretty hard to keep secrets from him. Anyway, we have more important issues to discuss than James Miesner or Charles Egan. How are you getting along with researching the World Court?"

Tyrell looked at his computer screen. "Well, it is comprised of fifteen judges of different nationalities. Now, until we get more information I don't know if all fifteen will preside over our case. They often use fewer, but I suspect that because of the importance of this case they will use all of them. I have a list of their names and I will study each of their backgrounds to see exactly who we are dealing with. The court usually doesn't deal with this type of case but are making a exception for this one."

Emma rose to leave and said, "Good, dig as deep as you can. The more we can find out, the better. Talk to you later." She left Tyrell's office and headed for her own, stopping briefly along the way to chat with Maggie.

As Emma rifled through some papers on her desk, Jeff appeared at her door. "Hi, Jeff, come on in. Have a seat."

Jeff Bulac was a tall, thirty-one-year-old lawyer with impeccable credentials for his age. He attended university in the UK as well as Toronto. He was strong in his faith and had goals that matched Emma's perfectly. Emma felt blessed that she had found someone so suited to her needs. Jeff was recently married and lived in the downtown area about twenty minutes from the office. Emma had met his wife, Isabella, a couple of times, and the two had hit it off immediately.

"So, how are you settling in?" asked Emma as Jeff sat down.

"I'm getting into the swing of things. The pace is quite hectic for a smaller law firm."

"Yes it is, and we have quite a substantial workload for our size and with the World Court case on the horizon; things are going to get much busier. That is why I am still looking for another associate, because Tyrell and I are going to be tied up with this other case for months. I realize that you are new, Jeff, but I'm counting on you to carry the load for a while."

"No problem, Miss Collins."

"Please, Jeff, not so formal. It's Emma."

He smiled and replied, "No problem, Emma."

They both chuckled as Emma said, "Okay, back to work!"

Jeff smiled and gave his new boss a half-hearted salute, and left her office.

Emma shook her head in amusement then returned to her work.

August 18

"Welcome, Reverend Nordstrom," said Emma brightly as she greeted her visitor outside of her office. "Please come in. It's wonderful to see you again."

"The pleasure is mine, Miss Collins."

Emma ushered Nordstrom to the plush sofa and then sat down in a nearby comfortable leather chair.

"How was your flight into Toronto?"

"Uneventful… just the way I prefer flights to be!" he said with a smile.

"Could I have Maggie get you some refreshments?"

"Coffee would be wonderful'" replied the reverend. "As I recall you offer some exquisite Colombian coffee in this establishment."

Emma chuckled and buzzed Maggie for the coffee.

"Now, Miss Collins, I cannot tell you how pleased the Council and I are that you have decided to accept this challenge."

Emma pursed her lips as she poured two cups of coffee. "I just pray that I can live up to your expectations, Reverend Nordstrom."

"We are most confident in your abilities, Miss Collins," stated Nordstrom as he opened his opulent leather briefcase and handed Emma a large brown manila envelope. "Now, I have prepared some written details for you; things such as times and dates and so forth. I have arranged for a woman by the name of Ingrid Swenson to act as our liaison. She will move to Canada temporarily in the near future and stay until your departure for The Hague. Ingrid will supply you with whatever you require, from airfare to security. Her contact information is in this package along with other vital information. Ingrid will be in touch with you within the next week or so to begin the process. Do you have any questions, Miss Collins?"

"So many, that I don't know where to begin," replied Emma, shaking her head as she skimmed through the information folder. "You mentioned security. Do you think security will be necessary?"

"Miss Collins, what you are about to embark upon is going to, shall I say, ruffle many feathers. There are individuals and governments who will consider you to be a great threat to them and their world. Your security is something the Council takes very seriously and we will spare no expense to see that you and your team remain safe. I do not mean to frighten you unnecessarily, but you must understand with whom we are dealing. Ingrid will be able to address any other concerns that you may have in the future." Nordstrom smiled and added, "Miss Collins, on a happier note, you will love The Hague! It is a beautiful city."

"I'm looking forward to experiencing it," replied Emma as she closed the folder.

"Very well then, Miss Collins, I will not take up any more of your time." Reverend Nordstrom rose and offered his hand to Emma. "We have total confidence in you. Ingrid will contact you in the near future, and I look forward to working with you and your team. Good day to you, Miss Collins."

Emma escorted Reverend Nordstrom from her office and then returned to her desk. She gazed out of her window for a moment, wondering just what the next few months might bring. Emma had difficulty absorbing the fact that her small firm would be defending probably the most high-profile case in history. She slowly shook her head at the whole idea of it, considering her humble beginnings. She opened her desk drawer and picked up the note. *Whatever it is, don't get involved!* She stared at the wrinkled piece of paper as a feeling of anxiety washed over her. Emma stuffed the paper back into her desk, picked up her office phone, and buzzed Maggie.

August 21

Office of the Secretary-General of the United Nations
New York City

Viktor Morozov sat at his exquisite antique oak desk as he pondered the current state of the world. A native of Romania, Morozov was educated in London and New York. At forty-eight years old, the former president of Romania rose to power quickly. He now sat as Secretary of the United Nations, one of the most powerful positions on earth. Morozov quietly contemplated how the world had changed since the pandemic; how countries had drawn further apart. Because of this, the nations of the world had agreed to increase the power and authority of the U.N. Morozov believed that his plan of a one-world government was the only way that humanity could continue to exist. He considered the upcoming ban on Christianity a crucial component of his quest for his new world order. Morozov reached for his phone and buzzed his secretary. "Send in Mr. Yankov."

"Yes sir," answered his long-serving secretary.

Moments later, Miroslav Yankov entered the office. "Mr. Secretary General, what can I do for you?"

"Have a seat," instructed Morozov.

Miroslav Yankov was the man that Morozov had chosen to lead the court case against Christianity. At fifty-three years old, Yankov was an accomplished attorney and shared the same views on the new world order as did his superior.

"So, what news do you have on our case?" asked Morozov, not bothering with any small talk.

"Well, sir, I have word that the World Council of Churches has chosen their representative, a small law firm based in Toronto called Collins and Associates."

"I've never heard of them," responded Morozov.

"Emma Collins is their lead attorney. A young woman in her thirties."

"Is that the best Nordstrom could do, a young woman from Toronto that no one has ever heard of?" asked Morozov with a sly grin. "What do you know of her?"

"Not much, sir, we are checking her background as we speak. But Nordstrom must see something in her. I'm sure he has the resources to retain the best legal team money can buy."

"I am certain he does," mused Morozov. "So there must be some reason he chose a no-name attorney. Nordstrom is no fool. Find out what it is and keep me posted. That will be all."

"Yes, sir," said Yankov as he rose from his chair.

"By the way, who do we have on the ground in Toronto?"

"We have a man by the name of James Miesner, sir. He has Miss Collins under surveillance at the moment."

Morozov looked at Yankov. "Can he be trusted?"

"I believe so, sir. We have used him before, and he has proven to be a valuable asset."

"Very well, keep me posted."

"Sir," said Yankov as he promptly left.

18

Madeline Rivera ushered Charles into James Miesner's office. "He'll be with you shortly," she said and returned to her desk. Charles sat nervously waiting for his boss to arrive. He tended to feel uneasy when Miesner called him into his office. James Miesner could be ruthless when things were not going his way, and at this time, Charles feared that things were indeed not going his boss's way.

"What have you learned, Charles?" said Miesner in a gruff tone as he opened his door and quickly made his way to his desk.

"Well, sir, Emma Collins is not an easy person to get information from. I've tried to be as forceful as I can without tipping our hand, but I haven't learned much."

James Miesner sighed heavily and sat back in his plush leather chair. "Maybe it's time we changed our approach," he said as he stared across the room.

"How so?"

"I think it's time to strike some fear into Miss Collins. I am concerned that she may just have the ability to sway the World Court. There *has* to be a reason why Nordstrom retained her, of *all* people. Let me tell you what I have in mind."

For the next thirty minutes, James Miesner laid out a plan to deal with Emma. Charles listened intently, somewhat unnerved at times by his boss's ideas.

"Secretary General Morozov's representative is demanding progress be made on this situation. He wants Emma Collins out of the picture as far as this case is concerned," said Miesner. "I'm not totally sure why they are so concerned about her, but we have no choice but comply with his demands. So, let's get at it! And keep me posted."

"Yes, sir, Mr. Miesner. I'll get on it."

"See that you do," said Miesner bluntly. "That'll be all."

Charles nodded and rose from his chair.

James Miesner stared at him icily as Charles hastened from his office. Miesner reached for his phone and hit number four on his speed dial.

Saturday, August 28

There was a hint of autumn in the air as Emma set out for her Saturday morning run in the park. Temperatures had cooled slightly in the city, making for more enjoyable running conditions. She silently thanked God for the fabulous weather for her run. Dressed in a powder blue jogging suit accented with navy trim, Emma inhaled the invigorating air deeply as she maintained a moderate pace on her way to the park. She quickened her stride as she came to the bike path that meandered through the lush green park space in the heart of the city. Emma loved her Saturday morning run; a time to clear her head of the past week's stresses and ready her mind for the challenges that next week would bring.

After twenty minutes of vigorous jogging, Emma slowed as she approached an unoccupied park bench. She uncapped her metal water bottle and took a sip of the refreshing liquid. She gazed out over the wondrous park, soaking in its beauty.

It didn't take long for that familiar voice to once again greet her as she relaxed on the bench.

"Emma, how are you this gorgeous morning?" asked the man in the well-worn Aussie hat.

Emma felt a slight tinge of excitement at the sound of Elazar's voice. She had begun to enjoy their conversations and his acute spiritual insights, especially as they pertained to her life. "Good morning, Elazar. Good to see you", said Emma with a broad smile.

"May I?" said Elazar as he motioned to the bench.

"Please do." Emma inched over to allow her friend a little more room.

Elazar wore his familiar long brown trench coat. "Another glorious day," he beamed as he gazed out over the immense park that was already bustling with activity; mothers with small children, people walking their dogs, and others just relaxing on the bright August morning. "It is good to be alive!"

The two friends sat in silence for a few seconds, and then Elazar turned to Emma, "So, how have you been keeping?"

"I'm doing well, thank you," she replied. "I do have some rather big news. You must be aware of the growing push throughout the world to ban Christianity?"

"Painfully," replied her friend.

"Well, I have agreed to defend Christianity in the upcoming court case in The Hague."

"That is marvelous, Emma!"

"I was approached by Reverend Nordstrom of the World Council of Churches recently and I agreed to take it on."

"Well, I do not think they could have made a better choice."

"It blows me away to even think about it. I never would have dreamed that a case like this was even possible. I pray that my firm can handle it."

"I have no doubt of your capabilities, Emma. The Council must feel the same way in order to offer you the opportunity to argue this case."

"The stakes are so high, Elazar. What if I mess it up?"

"As I said, Emma, the Council obviously has complete faith in you. On top of that, I believe that God has equipped you to fight and win this battle. Our Lord is using you for His purpose.

If He believes in you then who are we to dispute that? God is *with* you, Emma!"

Emma was enthralled with Elazar's words. A warmth washed over her as she had never experienced before. Any doubt in her mind about tackling this case had instantly dissipated. Elazar was once again proving to be a man like no other. His words reached down inside of her to the very depths of her soul.

"Something that is bothering me a little is that Reverend Nordstrom mentioned that he would provide me with security. He feels that there are forces that do not want me to succeed in this trial."

"He is correct in that. There are definitely forces that will come against you. You are encroaching on their territory and that will upset them. But keep in mind, Emma, God is with you. Do not ever lose sight of that fact. He will guide and protect you. So, do not be afraid to accept a security detail. The Lord will use those people to safeguard you."

Emma sat quietly contemplating Elazar's words of encouragement. She felt comforted by his wisdom. She realized that the time for doubt had passed, and from now on, she would have to immerse herself in this case totally.

"If you do not mind, I would like to pray with you, Emma," offered Elazar.

"Of course," replied Emma as she closed her eyes and shut out the sights and sounds of the busy park.

For the next ten minutes, Elazar prayed for his friend. He prayed for strength for her to face the challenges ahead. He prayed that God would stay by her side and protect her from all of her adversaries. He gave thanks that Emma had accepted this challenge and would not find herself overwhelmed by the upcoming court challenge's intensity. He prayed for her mind and body to have the stamina to see this trial to the end.

"Thank you, Elazar," said Emma when her friend had finished.

"My pleasure, Emma," he replied in a soft tone. "Now, go get them!" he added with a broad smile. With that, he placed his weathered Aussie hat firmly on his head and rose from the bench. "Good day, and may the Lord be with you, Emma Collins."

Emma stood and shook his hand. "Thank you, Elazar."

With that, the bearded man sauntered off into the distance.

20

Monday, August 30

The late August sun had retreated below the horizon by the time Emma had concluded her business in Stouffville, a town of about thirty-two thousand residents, forty-five minutes from her home in Toronto. She was clearing up some cases before turning her undivided attention to the looming court challenge against Christianity.

Emma turned her Envision onto Main Street and was suddenly blinded by the brilliant headlights from the vehicle following her.

"Woe, dim your lights!" she muttered as she adjusted her rear view mirror.

As Emma drove the vehicle behind her was creeping ever so closer to her. She adjusted her rear-view mirror to cut down on the glare.

"What's with this guy?" she wondered aloud.

Emma accelerated to attempt to put a little more distance between herself and the person behind her. As she did, the vehicle behind her followed suit and even gained on her. It now was following about five meters from the Envision. Emma increased her speed to seventy kilometers per hour, but within seconds the other vehicle had caught up to her. She tapped her brake pedal lightly to give her pursuer a warning, to no avail. She would be entering the highway in about two kilometers, so she pushed her speed up to eighty-five. The vehicle stayed with her once again. Fear had replaced anxiety as Emma saw the arrow for highway 404. She prayed that the vehicle would not follow her onto the highway. She turned onto the on ramp, barely slowing her Envision as she did. She struggled to keep her SUV under control as she navigated the One hundred and eighty degree turn onto the highway. Emma punched the accelerator and brought her Envision up to one hundred and thirty kilometers per hour. Glancing into her rear-view mirror she was horrified to see the other vehicle once again within a few meters of her.

Emma's mind was racing, trying to determine what to do. She wondered if this was a result of her taking the case for Christianity. She remembered what Reverend Nordstrom had said, that there were forces that would come against her. A chill ran down Emma's spine at the thought of it. She knew she would have to make a decision soon, in case this person meant to more than frighten her.

Emma could see a sign for the next exit. She was one kilometer from it. Her decision was made. She prayed quickly, "Lord protect me."

The exit came quickly. Emma held tight for the right moment. Her knuckles were white. She waited as long as she could, then at the precise time she pulled the wheel to the right and braked.

The trailing vehicle attempted to mimic her actions but it was too late for him! He passed the off-ramp and his front wheel caught the loose gravel, spinning his vehicle one hundred and eighty degrees and sending it backwards into the ditch. By the grace of God Emma was able to navigate the off-ramp at such a speed and safely come to a stop at the end of it. She turned onto the two lane highway and pulled in to a nearby service station.

Emma shut off her ignition and tried to catch her breath. Her heart rate was off the charts and she began to shake uncontrollably, wondering what had just happened.

After a few minutes she had regained her composure. She hit Tyrell's number on her screen. Emma explained to Tyrell what just happened.

"Sit tight and lock your doors, girl. I'll be there in twenty minutes," said Tyrell.

Emma pushed 'end' on her screen and waited. She looked around nervously, keeping a close eye on her surroundings, making sure she had not been followed.

Twenty minutes later Tyrell and Zahra pulled into the service station. Zahra jumped from her vehicle and ran to Emma, hugging her tightly.

"Are you alright, Emma?" asked Zahra.

"Yeah, I've almost stopped shaking," she replied, trying to force a smile.

"You didn't recognize the vehicle?' asked Tyrell.

"No, I think it was a pickup truck. All I could see were bright lights."

"Should we call the police?" asked Zahra.

"No point," replied Emma. "He'll just deny that he was tailgating me."

"I suppose you're right," agreed Tyrell. "Come on, let's get you home. Zahra and I will follow you."

†††

Tyrell peered through his boss's open office door the following morning. "Hey there, girl. How are you today?" he said calmly as he entered the office.

"Oh, hi, Tyrell. I'm okay, thanks. A little tired. Didn't sleep much."

"You know, Emma, you could take a few hours and rest."

"No time, we have too much to do," countered Emma as

she walked to the window to open the blind. "I called Reverend Nordstrom and told him what happened. I understand now why he mentioned a security detail for me. Scary! He said Ingrid would set it up for me. She is due to arrive at Pearson late this afternoon."

"I would like to stay with you until your security is in place," said Tyrell firmly."

"Yes, Daddy," replied Emma mockingly.

"I'm serious! I worry about you." Then he added, trying to repay her for her mockery, "If anything happens to you, then I'm out of a job!"

"You think that much of me, do you?"

They both laughed. They enjoyed the fact that they could joke with each other about serious situations.

"Okay, we have to get to work." Tyrell pulled a file from his brief case and placed it on Emma's desk. "Okay, this is what I have so far..."

Thursday, September 2

"May I help you?" asked Maggie as the visitor approached her desk.

"Ingrid Swenson to see Emma Collins," answered the short woman in her mid-fifties. Ingrid Swenson was an unassuming person who could easily be mistaken for an old fashioned elementary school teacher. She even sported a gold lanyard around her neck for her reading glasses. But those who knew her could testify that Ingrid was as hard as nails. She walked with purpose and exuded confidence in her speech. She had worked for the World Council of Churches for two decades and had climbed the ranks through her focus and tenacity. Those who knew her well would readily admit though, that beneath that tough exterior, Ingrid was a warm, passionate woman of faith.

Maggie rose from her chair in respect and said, "Welcome, Miss Swenson. Miss Collins has been expecting you." Maggie buzzed Emma's office and ushered Ingrid inside.

"Miss Swenson," said Emma as she met her visitor at the door. "Welcome to Toronto. How was your flight?"

"Uneventful, just as I like it," responded Ingrid with a chuckle. "And please call me Ingrid."

"And you can call me Emma. Could I offer you some coffee?"

"Actually, Emma, Reverend Nordstrom suggested I try your coffee. He said it was superb!"

"He *did* seem to enjoy it." Emma buzzed Maggie and asked for two cups of the fresh beverage. "Do you mind if my associate sits in on the meeting?"

"Not at all, I would like to meet him. Tyrell Lewis. Is that correct?"

"Yes." Emma said. She buzzed Maggie and asked her to send in Tyrell and a third cup of coffee.

Moments later Tyrell entered and smiled. Emma introduced the two and they sat down.

"So, Emma, I trust Reverend Nordstrom gave you an overview of what to expect over the next several months."

"He did and he said that you would provide me with the rest of the details."

"Yes, that is the purpose of my visit. I'm staying in a flat in downtown Toronto where I will work from." Ingrid opened her briefcase and removed two file folders. "Now I'll give you an outline of how things should proceed in the upcoming months and an outline of the security protocol that will be in place for your safety and the safety of your staff."

"On the subject of safety," said Emma, "I did have an incident this past Monday. I can't be sure if it had anything to do with the upcoming court case, but I think it may have." Emma relayed the details of the events of the past Monday evening. Ingrid listened intently, taking notes as Emma related her story.

"My goodness!" exclaimed Ingrid as Emma finished recounting the events. "It certainly would appear that the forces are at work already. Were you hurt, my dear?"

"No, just shaken up. My associate and his wife came to escort me home."

"Did you inform the local authorities?" asked Ingrid.

"No, I didn't get a plate number or a good description of the vehicle so I thought it wasn't much use calling the police."

"Do you have any idea who it might have been?"

"I have my suspicions, but I have no proof."

"I see," replied Ingrid. "Please inform me of any such occurrence in the future, Emma. My staff will thoroughly investigate this occurrence." Ingrid leafed through one of her folders and handed Emma an information booklet. "Here is a list of pertinent information and contacts that you can access starting immediately. Now, in light of your recent highway incident, I am posting security at your home and office. Also, Emma, you will be supplied a vehicle with a chauffer and security agent."

Emma nodded as an uneasy feeling enveloped her.

"Well, I believe that is all for now," announced Ingrid as she stuffed the files back into her leather briefcase. "Do either of you have any questions?"

Emma paused for a moment. "Not that I can think of at the moment."

"Very well, I'll be in touch. Thank you for the delicious coffee. I can understand why the reverend spoke so highly of it!"

The three rose and shook hands.

"Call me if you have any questions, either of you," said Ingrid as she smiled and exited the office.

Emma and Tyrell sat in silence for a moment letting Ingrid's words sink in.

"So, what do you think?" asked Tyrell.

Emma stared out of her office window and solemnly said, "I've got a feeling our lives are never going to be the same."

September 7

"Okay, I'll see you when you get here. Can't wait to see the both of you," said Emma excitedly as she ended the call. Her mother and Ben had just arrived at Pearson Airport and were picking up their rental car. Emma hadn't seen them in over a year and had been counting down the days until their arrival. She busied herself straightening up her small home in anticipation of their arrival. It was the day after Labour Day and the past four weeks had been hectic to say the least. She was looking forward to a couple of days with a lighter workload and spending some time with her mother and Ben. She understood that after these couple of days events would move at the speed of light. The tentative date of the case had been set at December 1. She thought it ironic that the trial would begin in the month that we celebrate the birth of Christ. They weren't actually referring to it as a trial, but in her mind Christianity *was* on trial and she would do all that was in her power to win this case. Emma paused for a moment to once again consider the enormity of her task. She still struggled to understand why the Council chose her to lead the defense in this monumental trial that could literally change the world. Emma sat on her living room couch, bowed her head and prayed, asking God for the strength and endurance to meet this challenge and be victorious.

Emma ended her prayer at the sound of her door bell. She scurried over and opened the door to the sight of her mother and Ben. Heather and Emma melted into tears as they embraced for what seemed like forever.

"I missed you guys so much!" Emma cried as she released her mother and threw her arms around Ben.

"We missed you, too, sweetheart," said Heather as she dabbed her eyes with a tissue.

"Come on in," said Emma as she helped them with their luggage.

"Your place is looking wonderful," offered Heather as they made their way into the kitchen.

"Could I get you some coffee or tea?"

"Coffee would be great," responded Heather as she and Ben sat at the kitchen island. "So, how are you feeling since your accident?"

"I'm okay. I was a little sore for a few days, but I'm fine now."

"Good to hear," said Ben.

Emma poured three cups of steaming coffee and sat down. "So, I have reservations for us tonight at a great Italian restaurant downtown. Tyrell and Zahra are going to join us."

"Sounds good," replied Heather. "How is Tyrell, anyway?"

"He's doing great."

"And his wife, Zahra, I'm dying to meet her."

"You'll love her, Mom. They are so well matched. She's really amazing! Reservations are for 7 pm."

The three talked over their coffee, catching up on what has been happening in their lives. Emma was anxious to hear about how things were in Regina and found herself a little homesick as Heather and Ben brought her up to speed on the latest news from her hometown. After their coffee was finished Emma showed them to her spare room to unpack and rest a little.

†††

A hint of autumn was in the air as Emma, Heather and Ben stepped from Emma's silver Envision in the restaurant parking lot. The evening air had cooled somewhat and the September shadows were getting longer. Summer was winding down in the city, making way for cooler fall temperatures. As the trio walked towards the restaurant, they were met at the door by Tyrell and Zahra. After introductions and a little small talk, the group entered the restaurant and were shown to their table. An amiable waiter took their drink orders and supplied them with menus.

"It's good to see you again, Tyrell," said Heather as they perused their menus. "And Zahra, it's wonderful to meet you!"

Zahra smiled warmly and Tyrell said, "Yeah, it's been a while."

"This is a lovely restaurant, Emma. Do you come here often?" asked Heather.

"Occasionally; I don't seem to have a lot of time dining out lately."

So tell us more about this case that you two are involved with," said Ben just as the waiter arrived to take their orders.

After the orders were taken Emma said, "Well, you must be aware of all the unrest around the word in the last year or so?"

"Yeah, it's scary. I don't understand what they are so upset about."

"Well," said Emma, "most of their anger is aimed at Christianity."

Heather asked, "Why on earth would they be so upset with Christianity?"

"It seems that there are some powerful forces that consider Christianity a threat; so much so that they want it banned completely."

"That sounds absurd," offered Ben. "It doesn't make any sense."

Tyrell spoke up, "Well, these people claim that Christian principles are keeping the world back from progress. They believe that these principles are out-dated and need to be abolished for the sake of the New World Order. Actually, this lines up with prophesy from the book of Revelation, that the world will someday see a one world government."

"What I don't understand," said Zahra, "is if it is prophesied in the Bible, then how can we stop it from happening?"

"We can't," answered Tyrell," but we must fight to hold it off as long as possible."

The conversation paused as their dinners arrived.

"Looks good!" said Ben as an assortment of Italian dishes were placed on the table.

"Tyrell, would you say Grace?" asked Emma.

"Sure." Tyrell prayed over the food, thanking the Lord for His blessings. When he finished they all dug into their meals.

"So, Emma, how did this all come about?" asked Heather.

"Well, I was approached by the head of the World Council of Churches some time ago. Reverend Nordstrom asked me if I would consider taking on the challenge of the case. I was completely blown away by the whole idea of it! I even asked him with all the lawyers in the world to choose from, why would he want me? He said that they had considered many people, but had decided on me because of my deep faith and commitment to what is right. They also considered the possibility that the opposing side may underestimate us because we are a small firm,"

"Well, I for one think that you two are up for the challenge," said Ben as he took another bite of his lasagna. "And don't forget who is on your side."

"So, Zahra, how long have you two been married?" asked Heather as she took a sip of water.

"About nine months. I immigrated to Canada about five years ago and met Tyrell a couple of years ago."

"Well, you make a lovely couple."

"Thank you, Mrs. Collins," replied Zahra with a huge smile.

"Please, Zahra, its Heather."

"So Emma, when is the trial scheduled to begin?" asked Ben.

"December 1, and I don't think the date is a coincidence. It is ironic, though; the month that we celebrate the birth of Christ. They had originally thought February, but it was moved up. Anyway, we have much to do before then. Tyrell and I are busy at the moment establishing our defense. If we don't win this case it will have grave repercussions throughout the world. I just cannot imagine a world where Christianity is not allowed to exist."

"So when do you leave for the Hague?" asked Heather.

"Around the middle of November. That will give us a couple of weeks to acclimate ourselves to the city."

"Will it be televised?" asked Ben.

"I believe so," answered Emma. "They're working on the details now."

"Well, we'll be watching!" added Heather.

Emma thought it best not to mention her security detail and the highway episode. She thought it would just cause uneasiness for her mother if she knew of the risk that she was taking.

After the main course was finished they enjoyed dessert and coffee along with some lighter conversation. Afterwards they left the restaurant, hugged, and promised to get together the next day.

September 11

Emma was greeted by brilliant sunshine as she stepped out of her house for her Saturday morning run. She realized that she would be leaving for The Hague within the next couple of months so she wanted to get as many runs in as she could. The difference on this day was that Emma had a running partner. Ingrid had agreed to hold off with security until Heather and Ben had left. Security agents were now posted outside her home and would accompany her on her runs. Today, Emma was joined on her run by a thirty-five year old agent named Adriana. Adriana was an eight year security veteran with the agency contracted by Ingrid Swenson. Emma found it uncomfortable at first, having a stranger run with her, but she soon felt at ease with Adriana's presence.

Emma's mother and Ben were on their way to visit Niagara Falls and then back home to Regina. Emma had enjoyed their time together but deep-down she was glad that they had left because of the mountain of work that she and Tyrell had to do in the next few weeks. Emma jogged slowly as her pony tail bounced in the light breeze. The September air blew softly on her face, prompting her to pick up speed. She entered the park and broke into a full run for the next few minutes, passing couples strolling leisurely along and others resting on park benches. After several minutes Emma slowed her pace and stopped to rest on an empty bench. She sat for a moment gulping down some cool refreshing water. Adriana stood a few meters away, constantly surveying the surroundings.

A familiar voice called to Emma from the distance. It was the unmistakable voice of the bearded man. As he approached the bench Adriana stepped in front of him with her hand stretched out toward him.

"Far enough, sir!" bellowed the security agent.

"He's fine, Adriana," I know him.

"Very well," replied Adriana as she cautiously lowered her hand to allow Elazar to approach Emma.

"Emma, how are you?" greeted Elazar with a broad smile as he approached. "And how are you, Ma'am?" he asked as he glanced at Adriana.

Adriana gave him a suspicious look; a look that she would give anyone she didn't know.

"Good morning, Elazar. You found me again!"

"To be perfectly honest, I hoped that I would meet you here today."

"Well, it is good to see you, Elazar," said Emma as she shifted over on the bench to allow her friend a little more room.

Elazar sat down with a sigh as Adriana resumed her vigil, standing close enough to Emma to protect her, but remaining far enough away as to not overhear her conversation.

"What a glorious September morning!" exclaimed Elazar.

"Yes it is," replied Emma as she took another sip of her cool water.

"I see that the Council has provided security for you. I am glad to see it," remarked Elazar as he removed his hat to wipe his brow.

"Yes, but I think it's going to take a little getting used to."

Elazar chuckled. "As long as you are safe."

Emma nodded slowly.

"And how is your case proceeding, Emma?"

"We're currently researching potential witnesses. We are looking at scientists, historians, clergy and professors." Emma paused for a moment and then turned to Elazar and said "You know, Elazar, I still wonder if I'll be able to handle this case. It is so crucial to the world. I really don't know if I am up to it."

Elazar pondered Emma's concern for a moment, "You mentioned to me some time ago that when you were younger you were told that God has a plan for your life, Well, I think that person was correct and that God's plan is beginning to unfold. I believe, Emma that God has chosen you for this challenge. I am convinced that you are the person He wants. So, if God is confident in your abilities, then should you also not share His confidence?"

Emma stared straight ahead and said quietly," Yes, I suppose you're right."

"I believe that I am, Emma. Now go with confidence and win this battle!"

"I will," announced Emma with a new enthusiasm. "Thanks for the encouragement, Elazar!"

"My pleasure, Emma," Elazar smiled as he placed his worn hat back firmly on his head. "I must be off." He rose from the bench, tipped his hat to Emma and smiled, "Until we meet again." With that, he was gone.

Emma sat for a short time and then nodded to Adriana, "Let's go home."

Part Two

THE TRIAL

24

November 1

The Air Canada Boeing 777 was packed full with sleepy passengers as it cruised high above the pitch-dark Atlantic Ocean. Emma and Tyrell relaxed in first class along with their security detail on the red-eye flight. They were due to arrive in Amsterdam shortly, and then take the forty-five minute train ride that would get them to The Hague. Emma was trying to rest, but sleep was illusive. She knew the pace would be intense once she got to The Hague. She stared out of the small window of the aircraft into the blackness and for a moment wondered if it all was real.

Upon their arrival at Schiphol Airport they were greeted by Ingrid along with their new security detail that was charged with safeguarding them during their stay in the Netherlands. Adriana and her fellow security agents would return to Canada the following day.

Emma and Tyrell were hustled into a waiting black SUV and whisked away to Amsterdam Centraal Railway Station to board a NS train to The Hague. Once they had reached their destination Emma and Tyrell were driven to the Movenpick, a luxury hotel located in the city centre. The Movenpick had opened in 2020 and would be home to the two attorneys for the foreseeable future.

Ingrid and the security detail along with the hotel manager accompanied Emma and Tyrell to their rooms. The manager assured them that they could simply call the reception desk for anything that they might need.

"So, I believe that is everything," said Ingrid to Emma. "You will also have a car and driver at your disposal. And of course, you must have security with you at all times. Alright, I will leave you to get some rest. There is a dinner planned for you this evening which Reverend Nordstrom will be attending. Your car will collect you at 7:30 tonight." Ingrid nodded and smiled warmly, then hurried from the room.

Emma laid down on her bed feeling exhausted. The overnight flight, the train ride and the stress of preparing her case over the last few months had left her feeling drained. She quickly drifted off into a blissful sleep.

The shrill sound of her room phone jolted her awake a couple of hours later.

"You awake?" said the voice on the other end.

"What? Yeah, I'm awake, Tyrell. I must have dozed off for a little bit. What's the time?"

"It's 6:30."

"Okay, I had better get a move on. I'll meet you in the lobby in forty-five minutes." Emma quickly unpacked the clothes she would wear to dinner and headed for the shower.

Promptly at 7:15 Emma met Tyrell in the lobby of the Movenpick Hotel. She looked elegant in her fashionable powder-blue dress with a matching shawl. Tyrell was attired in a tailored charcoal suit with a yellow designer tie, making the pair look very professional.

"You clean up pretty good, Miss Collins," remarked a grinning Tyrell as he rose to meet Emma.

"Not so bad yourself, Mr. Lewis. Ready for a night out?"

They both chuckled.

"Excuse me, Miss Collins, your car is here," said Max Peters, one of Emma's security agents. Max was a burly man of forty-two.

He had been a security agent for more than two decades and had protected many political figures and famous people over the years. He took his job seriously and would put his life on the line for any of his charges. At this moment his one and only concern was Emma's and Tyrell's well being. Max escorted his two charges out of the hotel's main entrance and into the waiting limousine. He scanned the immediate area for threats, was satisfied all was safe and then climbed into the front seat.

The dinner was lavish. No expense had been spared to welcome Emma and Tyrell. Ingrid Swenson met them as they entered the convention centre.

"Welcome!" beamed Ingrid as she escorted them to their table.

"Miss Collins! Mr. Lewis! Wonderful to see you both again," beamed Reverend Nordstrom as he rose from his chair to shake his guest's hands. "How was your journey?"

"A little tiring, but mainly uneventful," replied Emma.

"Uneventful; the best kind," joked the reverend. "This is my wife, Arielle."

"Einer has told me so much of the two of you," said Arielle as she smiled warmly. "It is wonderful to finally meet you both."

"Please sit," said Reverend Nordstrom as he positioned a chair for Emma.

"So you two are from Canada," said Arielle as they all sat down.

"Yes, Toronto," replied Emma.

"Lovely country; Einer and I have visited many times."

"Do you and your husband live in The Hague?" asked Tyrell.

"We actually live in the small town of Morgenstond, about four kilometers from the city."

The foursome was soon joined by Ingrid Swenson and her husband, Galen. The group enjoyed an evening of fine cuisine with a smattering of speeches, mostly welcoming Emma and Tyrell and forecasting a very difficult court case ahead.

November 2

The office was spacious, adorned with fine art from all over Europe. Miroslav Yankov sat behind his exquisite hand-crafted oak desk scanning his computer screen for important emails. Yankov's tastes were considered old fashioned by some, but he considered himself a man of culture. He refused to embrace current trends of furniture, hence the massive oak desk, as apposed to a more modern, sleek look. Miroslav Yankov was a tall man in his mid-fifties, physically fit and an extremely ambitious lawyer. He had been selected to represent the group of nations that was bringing Christianity to trial. He considered this case to be a stepping-stone to greater opportunities, as his ambition caused him to be constantly looking toward the future. He knew that the world would be watching the trial closely, and that it was his opportunity to express his atheistic beliefs while making himself a household name.

His office door opened just enough for his assistant to peer in. "Are you busy at the moment, Sir?"

"Come in, Leon. What have you got?" asked Yankov flatly, not bothering to look up from his computer.

Leon Hendrickson was the polar opposite of his boss. He was in his early forties and fifty pounds over weight. He lacked the ambition and ego of Yankov, but he was extremely efficient at his duties.

"Sir, I have the background information on Emma Collins that you requested," said Leon as he approached his boss's desk.

Yankov motioned for him to sit. Leon pulled a large folder from his brief case and handed it across the desk.

"I have never heard of this Emma Collins," muttered Yankov dismissively. "Where did Nordstrom find her?"

"Toronto, Sir," answered Leon with a slight smirk.

"Toronto? You mean to say that with all the resources at his disposal, the best that Nordstrom could do is ...a Canadian?"

The two men chuckled at the prospect of facing off against the unknown attorney.

Leon's face grew serious. "Sir, it is possible that this Emma Collins is much stronger than we think."

"Nonsense, Leon! Nordstrom is probably just underestimating who he is going up against here. Tell me more about our fierce adversary," said Yankov mockingly.

Leon opened his folder and said, "Well, she was originally from Western Canada, attended university in Toronto and actually scored top of her graduating class. She is currently thirty-one years of age and has a small law firm in downtown Toronto. She is single and has two associates; Jeffrey Bulac, who stayed in Toronto, and," Leon flipped to the next page, "Tyrell Lewis, who will sit second chair on this case."

Yankov perused the folder. "She does have a couple of impressive wins to her credit, but I am sure that she is no match for me. Keep an eye on her anyway, Leon. I don't want any surprises."

Yankov closed the folder and barked, "That will be all."

"Yes, Sir," replied Leon as he hurriedly packed up his brief case and exited.

Yankov sat staring ahead for a few moments as a menacing grin appeared on his face. He reached for his phone and punched his secretary's number.

"Get me James Miesner in Toronto." *Let's see if Miesner knows anything about Miss Collins,* he thought as he rubbed his chin.

Victor Yankov's secretary buzzed him a few minutes later. "Mr. Miesner on line one, Sir."

Yankov punched the 'one' on his phone and said curtly, "What do you know about Emma Collins? How much of a threat is she going to be?"

"Well, Sir, I believe that Miss Collins should not be underestimated. She may be young, but she is very driven. I did try to convince her to come on board with me but she refused. She has won some major cases in Toronto in the last couple of years, so I believe she will prove to be a worthy adversary."

Yankov frowned as he became frustrated with what he was hearing. "I think that you may be underestimating my own abilities, Mr. Miesner!"

"No, No!" exclaimed Miesner. "I would never, Sir!" he said, not wishing to offend the man. Miroslav Yankov was someone that James Miesner certainly did *not* want to offend.

26

The World Court of Justice
The Hague
November 15

It was a cool, crisp November day in The Hague. Emma's security detail climbed out of the jet-black Volvo SUV in front of the International Court of Justice building. After scanning their surroundings they gave the okay for Emma, Tyrell and Ingrid to step out of the vehicle. The two lawyers gazed in awe at the magnificence of the edifice in front of them, almost wanting to pinch themselves to make sure it was all real. One last scan of the area for threats by their security and then they were whisked into the cavernous building.

Once past security checks Emma and Tyrell were escorted to the courtroom where their case would be heard. Emma paused and stood spellbound at the sight of the grandiose room. She could still not quite grasp the enormity of the case that she was about to embark upon. The room was vacant at the moment making it appear larger than usual.

"I've never seen such an impressive courtroom," declared Emma as she continued to absorb the beauty of her surroundings.

Ingrid escorted them to a table where she invited her guests to sit. "Now, I believe that I sent all of this information to you some time ago but I would like to review it with you now." She removed several papers from her briefcase and set them on the table.

"Alright, the International Court consists of fifteen judges. Due to the significance of this case all fifteen will be present. At the end of the proceedings they will vote on the matter at hand. The ruling will be announced by their president, Justice Samuel Cardoso. The ruling will be final. Also, any of the judges can ask questions at any time. Most of the proceedings, you will be familiar with. Any questions?"

"I think we have it," replied Emma confidently.

"Excellent," said Ingrid and then proceeded too pack up her briefcase. "I will leave the two of you to it. I will call for a car for myself. Max and Adrian will return you both to your hotel when you are ready. Take your time; look around a bit if you would like."

With that, Ingrid made a call on her phone and then quickly left.

Emma surveyed the room some more, envisioning herself in front of fifteen judges arguing her case. She found mental preparation essential before a case, along with lots of prayer. After another thirty minutes they were ready to leave so Max and Adrian escorted them to the awaiting SUV.

Arriving at their hotel, Emma suggested they meet in her room for lunch and continue work on their preparations. With only about two weeks before the trial, time was becoming a valuable commodity.

†††

At noon they ordered room service of chicken wraps and salad. Emma cleared the clutter from the spacious table in her suite and the two lawyers sat down to enjoy their lunch and then dive into the work at hand. They discussed the background of all fifteen judges, trying to gauge how each one thought. Tyrell had worked tirelessly at amassing an in-depth biography of each judge. He and Emma discussed them all in depth for the next several hours before finally calling it a night at about 11 pm. They agreed to meet again for breakfast in the dining room at 9 am and get back at it. Emma wanted to discuss their witnesses and to confirm each one's intentions. Tyrell packed up his briefcase and slipped out the door to his own room across the hall. It was only 5 pm in Toronto so he decided to give Zahra a call before he went to bed.

Emma awoke about 7:00 the next morning and decided to take an early morning jog. She dressed in her pink and grey jogging suit and headed out of her room where she found Adrian standing guard. She tried valiantly to assure him that she would be safe alone, but he insisted that he join her. She knew better than to argue the point, so the two walked out of the hotel together into the cool, November air. They headed for a nearby park and made their way onto a bicycle path and began a slow jog. Adrian prided himself in his physical fitness and had no trouble keeping pace with the younger Emma. After about thirty minutes Emma spotted a park bench and suggested they stop for a brief rest. She sat while Adrian remained vigilant, constantly surveilling the surrounding area for any possible threats.

"Emma? Emma Collins? Is that really you?" said the man slowly approaching.

"Elazar? What on earth are you doing here?"

Adrian quickly put himself between Emma and the approaching Elazar. "Close enough," he bellowed, causing Elazar to stop in his tracks.

"It's fine, Adrian; Elazar is a friend of mine," said Emma.

Adrian backed away slowly, not taking his eyes off of the bearded man.

"May I?" said Elazar as he motioned to the bench."

"Of course," replied Emma as she slid over to make room for her friend. "But, whatever are you doing in The Hague?"

Elazar sat with a sigh and said with a sly smile, "Well, I heard that there was an important court case taking place and I wanted to witness it for myself. I thought I should experience the amazing Miss Collins in action!"

"I'm flattered, Sir!" replied Emma with a smirk.

"So how have you been keeping, Emma? I have missed our talks in the park."

"I am well, thank you. Tyrell and I are hard at work preparing for the trial." Emma paused and stared off into the distance briefly. "I sometimes wonder how our world ever came to this point, where Christianity would actually be on trial. I often wake up in the morning and wonder briefly if it is even happening."

"I agree, it is difficult to comprehend at times."

"And the lengths to which they will go to frighten me away from the case! I have been harassed; I have been almost run off the road. That is why I have security with me twenty-four hours a day."

"I am sorry to hear that, Emma," bemoaned Elazar, shaking his head slowly. "Have you ever wondered, Emma, why Christianity is attacked so fiercely? Why there is such a hatred for God and Christ? How a man such as Jesus was scorned and then killed because he claimed to be the Son of God? Evil in the hearts of man manifests itself differently in different times. That is why the love of Christ is so important. Two thousand years ago they tried to stop Him by crucifying Him. Today they are trying to stop you from defending Him. The task that you have been given is more important than any task ever given to one individual. Be safe, my friend." Elazar rose, tipped his hat and bade farewell to his friend. As he walked away he turned to Adrian and smiled, "Take care of her." Adrian gazed at the bearded man and gave him a half-nod.

The World Court of Justice
The Hague
Monday, December 6

It was a chilly December morning when Emma and Tyrell arrived at the World Court of Justice. Emma stepped from the SUV and again gazed upon the ornate building as she whispered a quick prayer asking God for the strength and ability to meet this enormous challenge that lay ahead.

"Good morning, Emma, Tyrell," greeted Ingrid as she met them at the door. "All set?"

"Ready as we'll ever be," smiled Emma.

"Excellent!" Ingrid escorted the pair to the courtroom. "May God be with you both," she said as she placed her hand on Emma's shoulder and then turned to take a seat at the rear of the room.

The press gallery was crammed full of reporters from every major news network throughout the world. This trial was proving to be the biggest international story in decades.

Emma and Tyrell took their seats and unpacked their brief cases. Emma busied herself studying her notes one last time. They whispered some thoughts and ideas between each other for several minutes until the call to rise was heard. It was an impressive sight as the fifteen justices entered the courtroom. The justices consisted of ten men and five women, all from different countries throughout the world. Emma and Tyrell had researched each and every judge thoroughly in an effort to formulate their approach.

Once all of the judges were seated, the chief justice began to speak. Samuel Cardoso hailed from Brazil. In his mid-fifties, Cardoso rose to the top of the justice system in his country through his intense work ethic and his unwavering belief in the law. He was known as a tough but fair judge, making Emma feel comfortable with him in charge.

"Good morning, ladies and gentlemen. Today we are embarking on a monumental case, which will have repercussions throughout the entire world. The case before us today is both remarkable and unusual. It is not the intention of this court to delve into religious matters normally, but these are hardly normal times. The world is currently at a crossroads and we believe we can aid in setting a course for the future of our planet. The court was originally reluctant to take on this case, but under the extreme pressure from many nations to resolve the issue, we decided that it is in the best interest of all concerned that we deal with it. Today, in this extraordinary case we find the Christian religion on trial. As I said, this trial will be different from what we are accustomed to, but it has been agreed upon by all nations involved that our decision will be final and binding. With that being said, let us begin.

Mr. Yankov, you may commence with your opening statement."

"Thank you, your Honour," said Victor Yankov as he confidently rose to give his opening remarks. Yankov was dressed in a finely tailored charcoal suit, crisp white shirt and lemon-coloured tie. He strode about with purpose, making eye contact with each and every judge. He believed that his style of delivery was as important as the words he spoke. "Your Honour, esteemed judges, it is the intent of the prosecution to prove that Christianity is a false religion, rife with fairy tales and silly fables. Not only will we prove that it is false, we will show how it has led to a whole range of societal problems since its inception." Yankov paused for effect. "Esteemed judges, the prosecution will show how Christianity, and for that matter, God himself, whoever He is, are total fabrications and have been scientifically disproved. Members of the court, we will hear from several prominent witnesses from the scientific community who will attest to these facts; witnesses with impeccable credentials to help us understand that this bogus religion has been the cause of much of the bloodshed and conflicts throughout history." Yankov paused again before he finished. "After hearing these testimonies, the court will have no choice but to rid the world of this insidious religion. It is not enough to ban it from our schools and businesses. Christianity and God must be banned from this world entirely, for the sake of everyone. I am confident that this court will make the right decision and ban this troublesome religion. Thank you."

"Miss Collins," announce the chief justice.

Emma rose and addressed the court. She was dressed in a striking navy blue suit with a bright white blouse. "Mr. Chief Justice, members of the court, thank you all for the opportunity to defend Christianity from these vicious attacks by the prosecution." Emma breathed deeply before continuing. "You have just heard the esteemed prosecutor, Miroslav Yankov, rail against Christianity, blaming Christians for all of the ills of this world, both past and present. Mr. Chief Justice, the defense will prove beyond a shadow of a doubt that Christianity is not only a legitimate religion and that God is certainly alive and well, but that God and Christianity are the only hope that this world has. We will establish three elements in our argument. First, that God does actually exist. Second, that Jesus did exist and still *does* exist. And third, that Christianity has not been responsible for the problems of this world, but as I said earlier, it is the ***only*** hope that this world has."

"Objection, your Honour!" cried Yankov as he jumped to his feet.

Emma turned quickly and stared at her opponent in disbelief.

"Mr. Yankov, you do have the right to object during opening remarks, but on what grounds?" asked the chief justice.

"Your Honour, the defense is already clouding the issue. She talks about three separate elements; God, Jesus and Christianity. She is already trying to confuse this court," argued Yankov.

Emma shot back, "Your Honour, it is impossible to explain Christianity without discussing God and Jesus. We will show how God and Jesus are obviously necessary for Christianity to even exist."

"I think the court can follow, Mr. Yankov, Your objection is over-ruled. Continue counsellor," he said as he motioned toward Emma.

"Thank you, your Honour," said Emma as she scanned the panel of judges and continued. "Again, members of the court, the defense intends to prove that Christianity is not only a legitimate religion but that it is the only true religion and must not be banned…truly, for the sake of this world. Thank you." Emma returned to her seat and breathed deeply, relieved that the opening statements were finished.

"Tyrell turned to her and whispered, "You raised some eyebrows with the 'only true religion' statement."

She turned and gave him a sly nod.

The Chief Justice jotted down a couple of hand written notes and then addressed the court again. "Mr. Yankov, you may call your first witness."

"Thank you, Your Honour. The prosecution calls Dr. Ashley Taylor."

Ashley Taylor rose from her seat and walked purposefully toward the witness box. Taylor was a highly regarded physicist who had written several papers opposing the Christian faith. She was single, in her early fifties. Her life was her work and her work was her life. Yankov considered her to be his prime witness. Taylor sat down after being sworn in and adjusted her microphone. She was fashionably dressed in a light blue skirt and jacket and exuded confidence with every move she made.

Yankov approached the witness box. "Good morning, Dr. Taylor. Please state your name and occupation for the record."

"Ashley Taylor. I am a professor of physics at the University of London. I've also authored several books, two of which are *The God Lie* and *Christianity Exposed*."

"So you are an expert on how the natural world works in general. How and why things are what they are. Would that be correct?" asked Yankov.

"Yes, I would say that I am," replied the self-assured doctor.

"Now," began Yankov, "on the subject of God, we are told that He created the universe in six days. As a physics professor and an expert in your field, what would you say to that?"

Taylor responded smugly, "I would say that that is preposterous! Utterly unthinkable! The earth and universe are so intricate that it would be impossible to be created in a few days. It has evolved over eons. It is *ridiculous* to think that it could be done in such a short time as a few days. For example, we only have to look at the animal kingdom to see evolution at its best. Just witness how animals have evolved and adapted to their habitats. Let me quote one of the most brilliant scientists who ever lived, Stephen Hawking. He said, 'The laws of physics and not the will of God provide the real explanation of how life began on earth'. According to Hawking, life began with a single cell and evolved over billions of years. The process of biological evolution was very slow at first. It took about two and a half billion years to evolve from the earliest cell to multi-cell animals and another billion years to evolve, through fish and reptiles, to mammals. But then evolution seems to have speeded up. It only took about a hundred million years to develop from early mammals to us. The reason is that fish have most of the important human organs, and mammals essentially *all* of them. All that was needed to evolve from early mammals to us was a bit of fine tuning."

"So as a physicist, what does this tell you, Dr. Taylor?"

"It tells me that in no way could the universe and life have been created in a few days. Just could not happen! So, as far as I am concerned, this ends any speculation of the need for a... miraculous god."

"Thank you Doctor," said Yankov as he shot Emma a wry grin as he returned to his seat.

"Your witness," said the Chief Justice as he motioned toward Emma.

Emma rose quickly and walked toward the witness. "Dr. Taylor, you have given this court a very eloquent account of the origin of life...but when you mention original single cells, I'm not sure I follow as to where these original cells came from. So Dr. Taylor, could you please tell this court how these cells came to be?"

Dr. Taylor shifted nervously in her seat, looking a little less confident than before. "Well, there is no definitive answer to that, only theories. The most probable theory is that life began in pools of chemicals called amino acids. These molecules would have been swirling around colliding with one another for millions of years until the perfect combination just 'happened'. You might say that it was the ultimate lucky break that started the chain of life! Another theory is that life started somewhere else in the universe and spread from planet to planet by meteors."

Emma turned to the panel of judges and said with a smirk, "So, I gather from your testimony that we humans are here because of sheer accident or because of... planet...surfing... meteors? Thank you, Dr. Taylor...Nothing further. Emma returned to her seat and couldn't help but notice a thinly veiled grin on Tyrell's face.

Ashley Taylor left the witness stand with a grim look about her as Justice Cardoso instructed Emma to call her next witness.

"The defense calls Dr. Caitlin Burke," said Emma.

Caitlin Burke was a forty-five-year-old, well educated woman who spoke eloquently and had the ability to capture people's attention as she expressed her views. She was dressed modestly in a grey business suit that denoted professionalism.

"Please state your name and occupation for the record," said Emma as she approached the witness.

"Caitlin Burke; I have a doctorate in religious studies and currently pastor City Christian Church in Vancouver, Canada."

"So you would consider yourself an expert on the existence of God. Is that correct, Dr. Burke?" asked Emma.

"Objection!" protested Yankov. "Your Honour, we have not established the existence of God, so how can the defense refer to this witness as an expert on something that doesn't exist?"

"Sustained," replied the Chief Justice.

"Let me rephrase, Your Honour," said Emma as she contained her frustration. "Dr. Burke, how much research on the existence of God would you estimate that you have done?"

"I have spent ten years and thousands of hours researching the existence of God. Three of my books delve into this subject in great detail."

"Tell the court why you became so involved in this research, Doctor," asked Emma as she paced slowly.

"In my younger years I didn't think about God very much at all," began Burke. "A good friend in high school talked to me about her 'experiences' with God; how He had 'healed' her brother of leukemia. Because she was a good friend I listened to her but didn't really believe it. A few years later I heard a similar story from another friend, so I decided to study any material that I could find on the existence of God. But first I wanted to study in a scientific manner. If I were going to believe in God, then He first had to make sense to me scientifically."

"And what have your studies revealed?"

"Well, there have been three great discoveries in modern science. **Number one:** physicists and cosmologists now believe that the universe began at a certain time from an infinitesimal, or zero point where there was neither matter nor space nor time nor energy…This points to a cause or creator that *transcends* space, matter and time.

Number two: physicists tell us about the fine tuning of the universe...laws and constants of physics are so delicately balanced to allow life to exist. For example, if gravity were a little stronger or the rate of expansion of the universe a little faster, life as we know it would be impossible. The entire universe is designed to maintain life on this planet.

Number three: embedded in every cell of all life is a DNA code which is the blueprint or instruction of life. Those who try to claim there is no intelligent design are absolutely at a loss to explain the amazing intricacies of DNA. Atheists will mock Christians' simple belief in an unseen God, but statisticians say the odds are utterly impossible that that such intricate code could just 'evolve'. In my view the only answer to the origin of life is a supernatural creator with intelligence far beyond anything we could imagine."

"What else does your research tell you, Dr. Burke?" asked Emma as she placed her hand on the witness box.

"As I said, all aspects of the universe point to intelligent design. Just take our planet earth, for example; we are the precise distance from the sun, 149.6 million km. Any closer and we would burn up; any further and we would freeze. In fact, the whole universe is finely tuned precisely to allow life to flourish here on earth. That tells me that there must be an extreme intelligence behind it. That tells me that God certainly does exist."

Emma motioned to the doctor and said, "Could you give us some more examples, Dr. Burke?"

"Certainly. When we consider life itself, we now know that the human body consists of about thirty - forty ***trillion*** cells. Now, Human Genome is the complete set of nucleic acid sequences for humans encoded as DNA. The entire list of three billion letters required to make a human being is contained within these cells. The letters are like instructions that are encoded in DNA. If human DNA were uncoiled it would stretch 16 billion kilometers! These are just a few examples of the complexity of the human body."

"Objection, Your Honour!" bellowed Yankov in frustration. "This is a court of law, not a high school science class. The defense is wasting this court's time with this useless trivia."

Emma shot back, "Your Honour, these scientific facts speak to the very basis of the defense's argument. They illustrate our position and confirm the existence of God."

"I'll allow it but limit it, counsellor," warned the Chief Justice.

"Thank you, Your Honour. Please continue, Dr. Burke," said Emma.

"Just a couple more illustrations of the complexity of the human body; the human brain contains eighty-six billion nerve cells joined by one hundred ***trillion*** connections. This is more than the number of stars in the Milky Way! Another astonishing fact concerning the complexity of the human body is that the human eye can distinguish approximately 10 *million* different colours."

Emma turned to face the panel of judges and said, "So Dr. Burke, in your professional opinion, what do these extraordinary facts tell you?"

"So much! But most of all, they prove to me that this universe and all that is in it is the result of an incredible intelligence beyond anything we can comprehend. In other words, God certainly *does* exist!"

Emma thanked Dr. Burke and looked at Yankov confidently and said, "Your witness."

Yankov rose slowly from his seat and approached the witness with a closed fist in front of him. "Dr. Burke, do you know what I have in my hand?"

The doctor hesitated, and then replied, "Uh, no, I don't."

"Why not, Doctor?" asked Yankov.

"Well, your hand is closed. I can't see what, if anything is in it."

"So you can't see it so you don't know for sure if anything does exist in my hand. Correct?"

"That is correct."

"Can you see God?"

"No, but I…"

"Yes or no, Dr. Burke. Can you see God?"

"Well…no."

"No further questions," said Yankov, sensing that he had just scored a point.

Emma shot up from her seat. "Redirect, Your Honour. Dr. Burke, does wind exist?"

"Of course!"

"Can you see it?"

"No, we just see the affects of wind."

"Would you say then that the same holds true with God? We cannot physically see Him, but we can see the affect that He has all around us?"

"Yes, that is a fair analogy."

Emma thanked the witness and returned to her seat. She gave Yankov a quick glance noticing that he was disappointed at the way the proceedings were unfolding.

After jotting down a few notes the chief justice nodded toward Yankov and extended permission for him to call his next witness.

Yankov rose slowly from his chair and said, "Thank you, Your Honour. The prosecution calls Dr. Reinhard Werner to the stand."

Reinhard Werner was a short man, slightly over weight, in his mid sixties. He wore thick glasses and though his English was quite good, he spoke with a thick German accent. His attire was, to say the least, modest. After being sworn in, the portly doctor made himself comfortable in the impressive oak witness booth. Yankov sauntered toward his witness as though he were formulating his first question as he approached.

"Doctor Werner, please tell the court what your occupation is," directed Yankov.

Dr. Werner shifted in his seat and began, "I am currently a professor of sociology at the University of Munich. I am also an author of several books which include *Is God Dead?* and *The Deceived Generation.*"

"Thank you Dr. Werner. Now... as a professor of sociology, tell us why you believe God does not exist."

"My years of research show me that God only exists in the minds of people. People who choose to look for an easy solution to life's problems. Now, to the *thinking* person, *man* is the ruler of his own destiny. You see, from the beginning of time humans have looked for purpose and meaning in their lives. Now, primitive man, with little knowledge and a low intellect, began using superstition as a means of explaining life and also explaining *his* reason for being. So, evidence that I have uncovered points to this time in man's development that he chose to...let us say, '*invent* God'. At this time humans did not realize that they themselves were actually gods and could chart their own paths."

"What else does your research tell us, Doctor?"

"Now, after humans invented God, it was relatively easy to keep the myth alive because no one could prove that God actually did exist. At that point the fables of Adam, Jesus, and Noah etc. began to circulate and the false religion known as Christianity grew from there. The scriptures were a compilation of fanciful tales from long ago with no actual relevance in today's society. I see absolutely no value in them."

Yankov paced the floor slowly, appearing deep in thought as he looked at the chief justice, "So, with your years of exhaustive research, in your professional opinion Dr. Werner, should Christianity be allowed to exist?"

"Absolutely not!" exclaimed Werner emphatically. "I believe that Christianity has been detrimental to the advancement of societies throughout the world for many years. Time and time again when a progressive society endeavours to advance in any societal way, then the Christian element comes into play and wants to put a stop to *any* advancement. They claim that morals should be steadfast instead of evolving with the wishes of society. And that is nonsense! I believe the Christian is a bane to society and his or her beliefs should absolutely not be allowed to exist, for the common good."

"Thank you Dr. Werner," said Yankov as he grinned menacingly in Emma's direction. "No further questions." Yankov returned to his seat confident that he had delivered a stunning blow to Emma's case.

Emma quickly made a couple of notations and then began to speak even before she rose from her seat. "Dr. Werner, you said that man 'created God'. Is that correct?"

"Yes indeed, that is correct."

"Well then Doctor, who created man?" asked Emma as she motioned to the court with outstretched arms.

Dr. Werner gained a puzzled look on his face. "I don't follow."

"It's a simple question Dr. Werner," quipped Emma. "Who created man?"

The doctor shifted uneasily in his chair. "Well...I…uh…"

"Objection! Your Honour, the existence of man is not in question. The existence of God is!" protested Yankov as he jumped to his feet.

"Your Honour, the question of who created man is integral to our defense," responded Emma.

"I'll allow it. Answer the question, Dr. Werner."

"Uh, what *was* the question, exactly?"

Emma stared at the witness for a moment. "Dr. Werner, who created man?"

"Well now, that question is really out of my field of expertise. I'm not sure that humans were actually *created* as such."

"So humans…just appeared…out of thin air?" queried Emma as she outstretched her hands palms up.

Dr. Werner was growing more and more agitated. "Uh, again, my field of expertise is human *relationship*. As for where man came from, I suppose he just...*appeared* on this earth... possibly from another planet. No one really knows!"

As a tiger stalking her prey, Emma pounced, "So you are asking this court to believe that we are all descendants of... space people?!"

"Well, I'm not sure..."

"Thank you Dr. Werner. Nothing further." Emma confidently returned to her seat as Yankov glared menacingly at the doctor.

"Next witness," said the chief justice.

"The defense calls Lucas Balaskas to the stand."

Lucas Balaskis took his seat in the witness stand after being sworn in.

Balaskis was tall, well over six feet, with an air of confidence about him. He was married and in his mid-forties. He was well dressed in a tan coloured suit, crisp white shirt and lemon-yellow tie.

Emma approached the witness. "What is your occupation, Dr. Balaskas?"

"I am an author and a Christian apologist. I also hold a masters degree in Philosophy."

"Could you explain to the court exactly what a Christian apologist is?"

"Certainly. A Christian apologist is someone who attempts to defend Christianity against objections. Our purpose is to answer questions pertaining to Christianity using reason and evidence."

"How then would you respond to the claim that mankind actually invented God and that He doesn't actually exist?"

"Good question" replied Balaskas with a smile. "We have to ask ourselves *this*; can we prove 100% that God exists. The answer to that is no, we cannot. But what we need is a certain threshold of certainty of His existence. We need to look at what is the best and most coherent arguments for the existence of God. We have to look at what is the most probable answer to the question of God's existence."

"Could you share some of those arguments, Dr. Balaskas?" asked Emma.

"Of course. Let me give you five reasons why I believe God exists.

Number one: Scientists now agree that the universe had a beginning. For many years the widely held belief in the scientific community was that the universe was eternal. So logically, and rationally it follows that if the universe had a beginning, then it had to have a cause. It is illogical to think that the universe could 'just happen'. So if you are an atheist, then you must believe that the universe just happened by accident, which is wildly absurd. Now that cause points to intelligent design, which in turn points to God. It's the only rational explanation. Now, many Christians believe that the universe is much older than what we originally thought. Science has indicated through the Hubble telescope that the universe began about fourteen billion years ago. They peg the age of the earth at about four and a half billion years."

"Doesn't that belief run contrary to what the Bible says, Doctor?"

"No. There is a now a belief that the seven days mentioned in Genesis were not twenty-four-hour-days. This can be justified in that even when we speak today we don't always speak in literal terms. For example, if I were to tell you that I witnessed a car flying down the road, you would immediately understand that I did not mean literally flying, but travelling at a high rate of speed. So we have to understand that we cannot always take literally what we hear. But the most important fact to remember is that whether the universe was made in seven days or fourteen billion years, God is still the Creator. Also, even if the earth is four and a half billion years old, God created man only a few thousand years ago. It goes against God's laws of physics that man could have developed and evolved from another form of life.

Number two: The fine-tuning of the universe. The universe has been incredibly fine-tuned in order to support life. Let me give you some numbers to illustrate how precisely the universe is fine-tuned. The number of seconds since the beginning of the universe is about 10(18). That's 10 with eighteen zeros after it; a ***huge*** number. The number of sub atomic particles in the known universe is said to be around 10 (80). Now, considering those numbers, in order for the universe to be life permitting, the force of gravity has to be fine-tuned to 1:10 (100). The expansion of the universe is fined tuned to 1:10 (120) Now, consider this; Roger Penrose of Oxford University has estimated that the odds of the universe coming into being by chance are 1:10 (10) (123)! To call this number astronomical would be a wild understatement! Any thinking person *must* admit that this is the definition of impossible!

Number three: Objective moral values and duties. Now, if God does not exist, then it is hard to find a moral standard for right and wrong; good and evil. Atheists believe that our morality comes from our evolution and environment. But the problem with this belief is that we do find some objective morality in our society. Even most atheists will believe that it is morally wrong to murder small children. We have to ask then, what is the foundation of objective morality? The answer to that, I believe, is God. He sets the moral standards. Without this moral standard then *any* behaviour could be morally acceptable.

Number four: The death and resurrection of Jesus. Most scholars have come to the understanding that Jesus of Nazareth came on the scene with an unprecedented sense of divine authority...The authority to stand and speak in God's place. To illustrate this, He carried out a ministry of miracles and healing. But the most radical confirmation was His resurrection. If He really did rise from the dead that means He must have been who He claimed to be and that God has publicly vindicated Him.

Number five: He is a personal God. You can know that God exists by personally experiencing Him. If you call on Him and accept Him, then He will answer your call and begin to change your life."

"Thank you, Dr. Balaskas," said Emma as she returned to her seat.

"Does the prosecution have any questions for this witness?" asked the chief justice.

"Yes, Your Honour," said Yankov as he rose slowly. "Dr. Balaskas, you say that morality comes from God. Correct?"

"Yes."

"Well, I know many people who don't believe in God, but are very good and moral people. How do you account for that?"

"I agree with you, sir. There are undoubtedly moral people who do not believe in God. But the point I was making was that only through God can we justify morality. If God does not set the moral standard, then who is to say that Hitler or Stalin, who were responsible for the murder of millions, were evil or immoral? Obviously their morality differed from most, but only through the Living God can we have a true moral benchmark. Only through the Living God can we ***justify*** our morality."

"But how do you account for the morality of unbelievers?"

"If God does not exist, then it is difficult to find any standard for morality. So for ***anyone*** to show morality, I think, is proof that a moral benchmark does exist, and that moral benchmark is set by God," answered the witness.

"No further questions, Your Honour."

"Court is adjourned until 9 am tomorrow," announced the chief justice as he banged his gavel.

Tyrell and Emma packed up their briefcases as they quietly discussed their first day. Glancing across at the prosecution they could see Yankov and Hendrickson were engaged in a very animated discussion. Neither appeared pleased with their first day. They were soon joined by Victor Morozov, who was obviously also displeased with their performance.

"I trust that the two of you will perform more competently tomorrow, gentlemen. Losing this case is *not* an option," he reminded the two prosecutors, not realizing that he was speaking loudly enough to be overheard by Emma and Tyrell. Morozov then lowered his voice and continued, “You both assured me that this case would be a slam dunk.” He glared fiercely at his two attorneys for a few more seconds and then stormed out of the court room.

Tyrell looked at his partner with a sly grin as they slowly walked toward the back of the court room, confident that their first day had been a success.

29

Sunday, December 15

Emma and Tyrell were enjoying a rare evening of relaxation at a downtown restaurant in The Hague. The trial had begun well so they treated themselves to dinner out. They dined on Dutch cuisine with a dessert of oliebol, a mouth-watering Dutch pastry. After enjoying a two hour meal they paid their bill and got up to leave.

Max Peters, one of their security agents had been watching over them from the front of the restaurant. He approached the pair to escort them home. His partner, Adrian Janssen remained in the SUV close by the restaurant.

It was a rainy, chilly evening, typical of December in The Hague. It had rained off and on most of the day and now it was definitely on! Max Peters led his charges from the restaurant, scanning the immediate area as they filed through the front door. Adrian Janssen had pulled up in front with the SUV. Tyrell held an umbrella over Emma in an attempt to shield her from the deluge. Max opened the rear door as he scanned the area for possible threats. Tyrell continued to do his best to shelter Emma from the intense rain.

A sharp crack was heard in the distance. Tyrell watched in horror as Emma's eyes roll back in her head as she slipped to the rain-soaked pavement.

"NO!" screamed a stunned Tyrell as he immediately dropped to his knees to attend to his friend. He raised her head onto his lap with one hand as he continued to harbour her from the rain with his umbrella. "Please, God, no!" he pleaded as he wept uncontrollably.

Max drew his side arm and scanned the area for the shooter. He then grabbed a towel from the SUV and directed Tyrell to hold it tightly on the wound.

"Someone call an ambulance!" screamed Tyrell.

"Faster if we drive her," retorted Max. He ordered Tyrell into the SUV, and then hurriedly lifted the injured Emma into the back seat so she could rest her head on Tyrell's lap. Max closed the door and jumped into the front seat. "Step on it, Adrian!" As the SUV sped off Max made a call to the nearest hospital. "This is Max Peters, UN security agent. We have a female, early thirties with a gunshot wound. Our ETA is seven minutes. Have trauma unit standing by. Number one priority." He clicked off his phone and turned to Tyrell. "How is she?"

"She's still…alive," he responded, his voice cracking.

The SUV raced through the rain-drenched streets of The Hague bound for the nearest hospital. Adrian Janssen was very familiar with this city and was able to navigate the streets like a Formula 1 driver, even in the rain.

"Are you keeping pressure on the wound?" asked Max as he again turned to Tyrell.

"Yes, but I don't know if it's helping."

"Come on, Miss Collins, stay with us!" encouraged Max, still aghast that he had let this happen. In his two decades of security work he had always managed to keep his charges safe. For a moment he considered his situation and came to the realization that his career would now be over. An event as serious as this would definitely result in Adrian and himself being fired. The stakes are just too high to let a mistake like this occur without there being consequences. This made him all the more bound and determined to keep Emma alive.

Max forced himself to get his mind back on the situation at hand. The SUV pulled into the emergency parking lot and was immediately met by the trauma team. Max hurriedly supplied them with as much information as he could as they placed Emma on a waiting gurney and whisked her away into the hospital. Tyrell demanded to go with her but he was ordered to go to the waiting room while Emma was assessed. He begrudgingly obeyed and made his way into the hospital waiting area.

The waiting area was almost empty, but he found himself unable to sit. He paced the floor, his soggy clothes stained crimson. Tyrell continued to pace and pray that his boss and friend would survive. He chastised himself for allowing Emma to be exposed in the street. *I should have been more careful!* He chided himself mercilessly, convinced that it was his fault. "Oh, God!" he cried, "let her live!"

†††

Max Peters nervously telephoned Ingrid Swenson with the tragic news. To say that she was angry would be a gross understatement.

"Mr. Peters, how could the two of you allow this to happen? You are both seasoned security agents! I am sure you both are well aware of the gravity of this situation." Ingrid paused for a moment and then added, "I am about twenty minutes from the hospital. I will see you then." She abruptly clicked off her phone.

Max looked at his phone for a moment then at Adrian. "She'll be here in twenty."

The two agents sat down solemnly and discussed the recent tragic event. They replayed it over and over trying to determine where they went wrong. Perhaps Adrian should have assisted in walking Emma to the vehicle. Perhaps more agents should have been assigned to protect her. 'What ifs' and 'maybes' dominated their conversation. After a few minutes the two agents just sat quietly waiting for their boss.

Several minutes later Ingrid Swenson and her aid strode through the front entrance of the emergency department. She didn't bother to stop and speak with her agents on her way to the information desk.

"May I help you?" asked the duty nurse.

"Emma Collins was brought to this hospital a short time ago with a gunshot wound. I need a report on her situation."

"Are you a relative, Ma'am?"

"My name is Ingrid Swenson. I am the special liaison between The World Council of Churches and Emma Collins. Miss Collins is currently the lead council in the defense of Christianity at the World Court."

"Let me check, Miss Swenson," said the nurse. Ingrid's tone left no doubt that she was indeed who she claimed to be. The nurse checked her computer. "Miss Collins is still in surgery. I'll have the doctor speak to you when he is finished."

"Please let me know the moment she is out. Thank you." Ingrid turned and spotted the two agents. She made her way over to where they were seated. "She is still in surgery," said Ingrid tersely. "I do not wish to discuss this matter any more this evening, but the two of you will report to my office at 8 am tomorrow. You are both excused tonight. I have to make a telephone call to Reverend Nordstrom."

The two agents quickly exited the emergency department with sullen looks on their faces. They now had to face the fact that their careers were almost certainly over.

†††

Tyrell stared at his watch. It was just past 10 pm. He calculated that it was about 2 pm in Regina. He wasn't sure how to tell her but he knew that he must call Emma's mother. He felt sickened by the thought. He pulled out his phone and punched in her number. His heart raced as he waited for Heather to answer. He tried with all of his might to keep his emotions in check as he spoke to Heather, but he knew it would be almost impossible.

"Hello?" said the voice on the other end.

Tyrell could feel his emotions welling up inside of him. "Mrs. Collins?" sniffed Tyrell.

"Tyrell, is that you? What's wrong?" said Heather with an uneasy feeling.

"Mrs. Collins….Emma is having emergency surgery."

Heather was about to collapse. "What!?"

"Mrs. Collins, Emma was shot tonight. She is in surgery at the moment," replied Tyrell, beginning to regain his composure. "I'm at the hospital now waiting to hear from the doctor."

Heather shrieked as she slid down into her living room chair feeling faint. "What did you say, Tyrell?"

"What's going on?" asked Ben apprehensively as he rushed into the room.

"How did this happen, Tyrell? I thought the two of you have security with you at all times."

"We had two agents with us. Somehow they missed the shooter."

"Ben and I will be on the first flight available to The Hague. Please, Tyrell, call me the second you have any news." With that Heather clicked off. "Oh, Ben, Emma has been shot! She's in surgery at the moment."

"Shot? How? Where?" replied a shocked Ben.

"I didn't get the details from Tyrell; only that she had been shot and is in surgery. I need to call and book our flight to Amsterdam."

"You rest," said Ben softly. "I will take care of the flight."

"Thank you." Heather bowed her head and began to pray.

Several minutes later Ben got off the phone to their travel agent. "Okay, we are booked on an early evening Air Canada flight to Toronto, then KLM red-eye to Amsterdam. We can catch a train from Amsterdam to The Hague. We should be there by 8 or 9, their time."

"Thanks, Ben," said Heather, somewhat relieved, but still feeling drained. "How could this happen, Ben? Emma's a lawyer. Why would anyone shoot her?"

Ben sighed heavily and said, "I fear that it has something to do with the case she is arguing. I'm sure there are forces that want her out of the picture. Allowing Christianity to continue has many people nervous."

Ben hugged his wife tightly as she began to sob once again. "We'll find out more tomorrow," he whispered in a reassuring tone.

The minutes turned into hours as Tyrell waited nervously for word from the surgeon. He paced the floor, then prayed, and then paced some more. He checked the clock above him; 2 am. He wasn't sure if such a long time in surgery was a good sign or bad. *At least she is still alive.* He felt sickened that his closest friend was fighting for her life and there was nothing he could do but wait and pray. Psalm 145; 18 came to mind as he sat quietly "*The Lord is near to all who call upon Him; to all who call upon Him in truth.*" Tyrell felt comforted by this scripture. He once again bowed his head.

"Mr. Lewis?" asked the approaching physician.

Tyrell sat upright immediately and glanced at his watch. 2:27 am "Yes, Doctor, hello."

"I'm Doctor Jansen. I was told that you are close to Miss Collins,"

"Yes, we're from Canada and are currently working on a case in The Hague," replied Tyrell. "So, how is she?"

The surgeon sat down beside Tyrell and explained, "Now, the surgery went as well as could be expected. Obviously, Miss Collins suffered very serious injuries. She was hit by only one bullet, but it caused significant damage. The bullet grazed her neck and lodged in her left shoulder. First of all, she was extremely lucky that the bullet did not strike her neck an inch or two to the right; otherwise your friend would not be with us any more."

Tyrell hung his head, thanking God for His mercy. "I wouldn't call it luck, Doctor."

"Yes, well, be that as it may, Miss Collins came through the surgery quite well. The bullet lodged in her left humerus. That's the bone in the upper shoulder. I repaired the damage to the bone after removing the bullet. She should recover fully, but will need extensive physio for her shoulder," explained Dr. Jansen.

"When can I see her, Doctor?" asked Tyrell as his voice cracked.

"She's in intensive care and is heavily medicated. Possibly in a few hours you will be able to say a quick 'hello'. If you will excuse me, I will check in on her later." With that, Doctor Jansen briskly walked away and disappeared into his next patient's room.

Tyrell shook his head slowly as he slumped down into his chair. *How did this happen? Where do we even go from here?* These were just a couple of the questions that flooded his mind.

†††

As Tyrell sat quietly in the common area near the surgical ward he was awakened by the voice of Ingrid Swenson. "Mr. Lewis, any word?" she said as she approached. Ingrid was accompanied by a solemn-looking Reverend Nordstrom.

"I'm so sorry about your colleague, Mr. Lewis" said the reverend as he offered his hand to Tyrell.

Tyrell quickly rose and shook his hand. "Thank you, Reverend. I spoke with the surgeon a while ago. He said Emma came through the surgery well, but will require extensive rehabilitation."

"Thank God she survived," said Nordstrom as he sighed deeply. "Did her doctor say when we will be able to visit her?"

"Possibly a short visit in a few hours; she's still heavily sedated. Who would do this to her?" asked Tyrell as he once again became filled with emotion.

Reverend Nordstrom motioned to Tyrell to sit back down as

he and Ingrid sat down beside him. "Son, I am afraid that there are powerful forces working against us that will stop at nothing to ensure that we are not successful in this trial. The stakes are that high!"

"What happens now with the trial?" asked Tyrell despondently.

"I will speak with Miss Collins when she is feeling better and ask her is she wishes to proceed or not. In the mean time I will ask the court for a continuance," replied Nordstrom. "Has her family been notified?"

"They will be here in a few hours."

"If there is anything you need, please let Ingrid know," said the reverend as he placed his hand on Tyrell's shoulder.

Tyrell nodded slowly and stared off into the distance, still trying to come to terms with all that had happened in the last few hours. *Scaring her on the highway wasn't enough so they tried to* ***kill*** *her?* Disturbing thoughts raced through his mind as he contemplated what had transpired. He dreaded the thought of facing Emma's mother when she arrived later in the day.

Office of James Miesner
Toronto, Canada
December 16
8:30 am

Madeline Rivera buzzed her buss's office. "Sir, Charles Egan on line 2."

Miesner punched the '2' on his phone. "What is it, Charles?"

"Have you heard the news?" asked Charles with some urgency.

"What news?"

"Emma Collins was shot last night leaving a restaurant in The Hague."

There was silence for a moment on the other end. "Is she…?"

"She's alive. She's in intensive care at the moment. That's about all I know at this time."

"Keep me posted on any developments," said Miesner quietly as he gently replaced his receiver. He sat for a moment in sheer disbelief. "What were they thinking?" he said to himself. "I knew they wanted to silence her, but to *shoot* her? They must be mad!" Miesner picked up his phone once again and dialed an overseas number.

"Yes?" came the voice on the other end.

"What in blazes is going on over there!?" asked Miesner harshly. "What were you thinking?"

The voice on the other end shot back, "We are handling things over here."

"I heard how you are handling things! Nothing was said to me about resorting to attempted murder," responded Miesner sharply. "I want no part of that!"

"You are already part of it, Mr. Miesner," said the voice in a matter of fact tone. "You are in it up to your neck."

"We'll see about that!" snarled Miesner, seething with anger as he slammed the receiver down. He sat for a moment as he collected his thoughts and then rose from his chair and left his office.

"I'm going out!" Miesner snapped as he hastened by Madeline's desk. Madeline looked at her boss in bewilderment as he passed.

"Should I forward your calls?" asked the confused secretary.

No answer was given as Madeline watched the large door close behind her boss. She shuddered to think of what might be going on. Clearing her mind of the possibilities, Madeline continued on with her duties. She had often wondered just what her boss might be involved in but then concluded that she was probably better off not knowing.

The duty nurse quietly approached Tyrell as he dozed in the uncomfortable hospital waiting room chair. She gently placed her hand on his shoulder, waking him with a start.

"Sorry to wake you, Mr. Lewis, but Doctor Jensen says you can visit Miss Collins for a few moments."

"Thank you, nurse," replied Tyrell as he rubbed his eyes in an effort to sooth them.

"I'll show you to her room," offered the nurse as she motioned to Tyrell.

Tyrell followed her down the long hospital corridor to the intensive care unit. He was ill prepared for the shock of seeing Emma lying in the bed with an array of wires and hoses protruding from her body. Tyrell wept silently at the sight of his wounded friend. A flood of memories rushed through his mind…memories of college days…memories of the early days of their careers. He gently held her hand as he wept quietly.

"I'm so very sorry for letting this happen," whispered Tyrell. "I should have been more careful." Tyrell prayed silently for a few minutes for his friend. He thought he noticed her eyes flutter for a moment as though she was awakening, but they remained closed. The nurse returned a few minutes later and suggested to Tyrell that he let Emma rest and come back later.

"I'd like to sit with her for a while, if I could," said Tyrell softly.

The nurse placed her hand on his shoulder and said, "I suppose it wouldn't hurt for a while. Not too long, though," she added with a smile. I'll tell the security officer by the door that you will be staying. Tyrell nodded and pulled up a chair to sit by Emma's bed. He glanced at his watch; 4:08 am. He once again began to pray for his friend. *She looks so vulnerable as she lay on that hospital bed,* he thought as he finally succumbed to exhaustion and drifted off to sleep.

Tyrell awoke about four hours later. His body ached from the uncomfortable hospital chair. He slowly turned his head in an effort to loosen his neck and then slowly stood to stretch his fatigued muscles. Emma continued to sleep as the bedside monitors hummed softly. Tyrell touched her hand gently and then decided to search for a cup of coffee.

Tyrell returned several minutes later with a steaming cup of coffee and a light snack. He took a sip of coffee and a bite of an apple Danish. *Hospital food has never tasted so good*, he thought as he took another bite. He sat back down, feeling a little better. Tyrell finished his Danish and then looked over at Emma. Just at that moment he thought he saw Emma's eyes flicker.

"Emma, can you hear me?" said Tyrell as placed his cup on a nearby table. "Emma?" he whispered once again. There was no sign of movement. He sighed and then sat back in his chair.

Tyrell closed his eyes once again and tried to sleep. He suddenly awoke to a feeble sound coming from Emma's direction. He sat upright and said, "Emma?"

"Tyrell? Where am I?" Emma slowly opened her eyes and peered at Tyrell.

"We're still in The Hague, but you're in the hospital. You were shot last night; outside the restaurant."

A look of shock appeared on Emma's face. "What?"

"Yeah, when we were leaving the restaurant, but the doctors say you'll be okay. You just need some rest. Your mother and Ben are on their way over; they should be here soon."

Emma stared at the ceiling with a perplexed look on her face. She was having difficulty coming to terms with the fact that someone had actually shot her. As she contemplated Tyrell's words tears formed in her eyes.

"Why would someone do this?" she asked as she continued to stare at the ceiling.

Tyrell smiled and said comfortingly, "Look, we can talk about this later. I'll tell the nurse you are awake. Be right back." He left the room in search of the attending nurse.

Moments later he returned with a smiling nurse. "Good morning, Emma; how are you feeling?" said the sanguine nurse. She checked Emma's IV and vitals and seemed pleased with her findings. "I'll tell Doctor Jensen that you are awake. Be right back."

A few minutes later the nurse returned with the doctor. "Good morning, my dear. You've had quite a night!" declared Doctor Jensen.

"So I hear," replied Emma softly as she regained her wits.

Doctor Jensen studied her chart and said, "Everything looks good, so you just rest and we'll talk later, okay?"

Emma forced a smile and nodded gently as her physician spoke with the nurse for a moment, smiled and left the room.

33

The KLM 787 landed smoothly at Schiphol airport at 9:07 am local time. Even though the flight was uneventful, Heather was unable to relax with the worry of her daughter's plight playing on her mind. As they entered the terminal they were met by a young man holding a card with Heather's name on it.

"Mrs. Collins? Good morning. My name is Erik Bakker." He presented his identification. "I have been instructed by Ingrid Swenson to collect you and drive you directly to the hospital and then to your hotel. I will help you gather your luggage and then we can be on our way."

"Thank you, Mr. Bakker. This is very much appreciated," said Heather, relieved that they wouldn't have to bother with a taxi or train.

The air was crisp, but much more comfortable than the sub-zero temperatures of Regina.

They arrived at the hospital about an hour later. The trip had been a quiet one, no one knowing exactly what to say.

"Here is my number," said Erik as he handed Heather a slip of paper. "Call when you wish to be taken to your hotel."

Heather and Ben thanked the young man and hurried inside.

Ingrid was waiting just inside the door. "Mrs. Collins, welcome to The Hague. My name is Ingrid Swenson."

"This is my husband, Ben."

Ingrid greeted Ben with a smile and a handshake. "Allow me to take you to your daughter's room," she said. "Follow me, please." They stepped inside a nearby elevator and headed for the third floor. "Emma has just now been moved from the ICU into a private room," said Ingrid as she led the way from the elevator. Heather's heart skipped a beat as she noticed the two armed guards outside Emma's room. *Is this the reality now; armed guards?* she thought as they drew closer to her daughter's room. Heather entered the room and gasped as the sight of Emma once again in a hospital bed evoked memories of her accident years before. This circumstance was so much more troubling because it had been intentional.

"I have a question, Miss Swenson," said Heather as she stopped in the hallway before reaching Emma's room.

"Of course, what is it, Mrs. Collins?"

Heather assumed a more solemn expression on her face. "Miss Swenson, my daughter came over here to fight a case in court. How is it that she ended up getting shot? I was under the impression that she had ample security, and now she is lying in a hospital bed!"

"My humblest apologies, Mrs. Collins. The security issues have been dealt with. The agents assigned to your daughter have been relieved of their duties. We should have done a better job of protecting her. Mrs. Collins, we are fighting forces in this trial that will stop at nothing to win. Emma presents a great threat to them because she is such a gifted attorney. They are truly fearful of her. I know that is of little comfort to you at this time, but you should be extremely proud of you daughter."

Heather slowly shook her head and said, "I'd like to see her now."

"Of course, follow me," said Ingrid softly as she led them to Emma's room. Ingrid nodded at the security agents guarding Emma's room and they promptly opened the door for the visitors.

Heather forced a smile as she said softly, "Hi sweetheart, how are you feeling?" The words were no sooner out of her mouth than she realized how thin the question was. She took hold of Emma's hand and held it tightly. "Hi, Tyrell," said Heather as Tyrell rose to greet the couple.

They visited for a while as Tyrell filled them in on all the details of the events of the previous night.

"You look exhausted, Tyrell, said Heather. "We can stay if you want to go to your hotel and rest."

"I think I will," answered Tyrell, struggling to stay awake. "I'll let the three of you visit. I'll see you all later." As he was leaving the room Doctor Jensen appeared.

"Good morning," said the doctor as he entered. "You must be Emma's parents."

"Heather Collins; this is my husband, Ben Alvarado." They shook hands and then Doctor Jensen examined Emma's chart. For the next fifteen minutes they discussed Emma's situation while the surgeon outlined the process for physio on her shoulder.

"Any questions?" asked the doctor. "Okay, then I will be back later to check on you, Emma." With that, Doctor Jensen left the room.

After the doctor was gone Heather's demeanor became much more fearful. She wanted to avoid a strained conversation with Emma at this time. Heather was afraid that her daughter would want to continue with this case after she recuperates. The thought of that was chilling. She decided to keep the conversation as light as possible until Emma was feeling better. The three talked for a little while longer until Emma finally succumbed to the affects of her medication and drifted off to sleep.

James Miesner turned his jet-black Escalade into the almost empty parking lot of his business associate and screeched to a stop in an open parking spot. He had partnered with Harold Mason on and off over the last few years. The two men loathed each other, but their lust for money and power created somewhat of a bond between them.

"I need to see Harold," demanded Miesner as he burst through the front door.

"I'll tell him you're here," said his secretary as she reached for her phone.

"Don't bother," hissed Miesner as he stomped through the reception area towards Mason's office. He entered without knocking and demanded, "What's going on, Harold?"

Mason looked up from his computer and responded curtly, "What are you talking about, James? Where do you get off busting into my office like that?"

"I'm talking about Emma Collins and the fiasco over in The Hague. Why was she shot?"

"Take a seat, James."

Miesner sat in a nearby chair and said, "I'm waiting."

Mason closed his lap top and looked straight at Miesner. "Look, I didn't know they were going to pull something like that. I was under the impression that they just wanted to scare her." Mason paused and took a deep breath before continuing. "You know as well as I do, James, that there are powerful forces out there that do not want Emma Collins to win this case. These forces will stop at nothing to get their way."

"Did they intend to eliminate her or just scare her?" asked Miesner.

"I'm not sure. I am not privy to all of their plans. I can tell you with some certainty though that they are not finished. Their objective is clearly to prevent the pro-Christian side from winning."

Miesner shook his head slowly and said, "Why, Harold? Why are they bent on stopping Christianity?"

"Well, my understanding is that Christianity scares them. Without Christianity in the world they would be free to conduct their business dealings any way they choose. That's my understanding, anyway. Your part in this is small so I wouldn't worry too much, James."

"That's funny, because when I called Europe about it I was told that I was up to my neck in it."

Harold shook his head. "As long as you keep quiet you should be alright. They're just trying to scare you. The only problem with you is that they are upset that you down played the abilities of Emma Collins. I can tell you that they are not happy about that. They had expected a more thorough expose on her."

"Well, no one had ever heard of her. How could we take her seriously?"

"They're taking her seriously now," responded Mason as he rose from his chair to signal that the meeting was over. "Just keep quiet and you should be okay."

Miesner sat for a moment and then said quietly, "Anyway, I know things about a lot of people involved in this. If I go down I will take others with me." With that said, he abruptly got up and left.

Mason watched his partner leave and then slowly shook his head and said soberly, "That guy is finished." He reached for his phone and punched in a familiar number. "It's Mason; we have a problem…"

After a couple of hours of rest Heather and Ben decided to visit the hospital again hoping that Emma would be awake.

Hi, honey," said Heather as they slipped into the hospital room. "How are you feeling?"

"A little better," answered Emma with a faint smile.

Heather acknowledged Tyrell, who was sitting in a chair on the opposite side of the bed. He had refused to leave her side.

Tyrell got out of his chair and offered it to Heather. "I'll leave and let you visit."

"Nonsense, Tyrell," replied Heather. "You are Emma's dearest friend and you are welcome to stay as long as you want." Tyrell nodded in appreciation and sat back down. Ben retrieved a chair from the hallway and the three of them sat.

"How's the food?" asked Ben, trying to lighten the mood.

"Not great, but I haven't really felt much like eating."

"Maybe I could slip out and pick you up a pizza."

"Sounds good, Ben," she said with a laugh and then she grimaced. "It hurts when I laugh."

"Okay, no more jokes." He replied with a chuckle.

There was silence for a few moments until Emma said, I wonder what will happen with the trial."

"Reverend Nordstrom said that he was going to request a continuance," said Tyrell.

Heather was unable to mask her fear anymore and blurted out, "Well, I hope you are not going to continue with the case!"

Emma stared at her mother in disbelief. "Of course I want to continue."

"Emma, look what has happened to you. You're lucky to be alive! How can you possibly want to continue this madness?" said Heather, shaking her head.

"Mom, you know the importance of this case. You've been a Christian for a lot of years. You understand the world wide movement against it."

"I do, honey, but I also value my daughter's life and well being. You have been through much trauma in your life and I'm just trying to protect you."

"I appreciate that, Mom, but I have to do this. I believe that this is God's plan for me and I have to follow it through. I hope that you can understand."

Heather had hoped to avoid this conversation until Emma was stronger so she thought it best now to defer this conversation to a later date. "Look, honey, we can discuss this when you are feeling better," she said with a smile.

"Okay", said Emma, sounding a little annoyed. "I'm kind of tired right now. I think I'll try to sleep for a while."

"Okay, honey, we'll let you rest," Heather said softly as she squeezed her daughter's hand. "We'll see you later."

Heather almost broke down as they made their way to the elevator. "Well, I certainly blew that!" she said, scolding herself. "How could I be so thoughtless? I didn't want to bring that up until she was feeling better. Now she is angry with me." Heather shook her head in disgust as Ben punched in the floor number.

"Don't blame yourself for being a caring parent," urged Ben. "Emma understands that you have her best interest at heart. She understands that you are simply a loving parent looking out for her daughter; just give her a little time."

Heather nodded slowly as the elevator reached the main level.

December 16
7pm

James Miesner turned onto the highway toward his home. The December sky was moonless with a sinister look about it. Miesner thought to himself that the bleak sky fit his current mood. All day long he had been rehashing his conversation with Harold Mason the previous day. He felt like the walls were closing in on him and he had to do something in order to rectify the situation. He drove on into the gloomy night weighing his options. He was well aware that everyone involved in this scheme would not survive until the end. It appeared to him that it was coming down to 'every man for himself'.

Miesner continued on until he reached a familiar curve in the road. At almost ninety degrees, the turn could be dangerous for a driver not paying attention. Being very familiar with this road, he approached the curve without slowing down as much as he should have. The curve rounded an embankment with a thirty meter drop down a jagged hillside. Miesner touched his brakes to begin slowing his SUV. A chill raced down his spine as he felt the sponginess of his brakes. He pressed harder on the pedal without any success. *What's going on?* he thought as the guard rail was closing in on him. He was travelling faster than he should have been, going into this curve. He put his foot to the floor to no avail and screamed as he broke through the guard rail and plummeted down the jagged embankment.

†††

Office of Harold Mason
Toronto, Canada

Harold Mason picked up his phone, "What?"

"It's done," said the voice on the other end.

Mason clicked off his phone and slowly placed it on his desk. He stared straight ahead emotionless.

37

December 17

"Good morning, Miss Collins," said Ingrid Swenson as she and Reverend Nordstrom entered her hospital room. "How are you feeling this morning?"

"A little better, thank you", replied Emma as she adjusted her bed in order to sit up. "Please sit down."

"Thank you," said Ingrid as she and the reverend made themselves comfortable.

Nordstrom looked at Emma sadly and said, "On behalf of the World Council of Churches I want to extend our apologies for this appalling occurrence. There was a failure in our security protocols and we are working furiously to amend them."

Nordstrom nodded to Ingrid to continue the conversation.

"Miss Collins, the World Court has granted a continuance in the trial. Now, we realize that you have been through a severe trauma recently, but I have to ask whether or not you intend to proceed with the case."

"I have no intention to back out," replied Emma emphatically. "I understand the importance of this case and the ramifications if we lose."

"That is wonderful to hear, Miss Collins," said Reverend Nordstrom. "Your faithfulness is an absolute blessing."

"What we suggest, Miss Collins, if you would like, is that you return to Canada for a time to recover from your injury. We will arrange our private jet to fly you and your family to Toronto and then collect you when you are ready. That way we can ensure your safety. You will also have a full security detail while in Canada."

"Thank you, I would like that. The doctor said I should be able to leave the hospital in a couple of days," said Emma.

"Wonderful, then I will have Ingrid make the necessary arrangements," said Nordstrom as his expression grew somber. "We are truly sorry that this tragic event occurred, Miss Collins." You have my word that your security will be enhanced to prevent a similar occurrence in the future."

Emma just smiled and nodded slightly.

"I will contact you tomorrow with the travel details," said Ingrid as she and Nordstrom said their good-byes and left the room.

December 18

The Leer jet landed smoothly on the runway at Toronto's Pearson Airport at 6:15 pm. The passengers had enjoyed the flight in the luxury jet.

"Beats travelling commercial," quipped Tyrell as he leaned over to Emma.

"You know it!" replied Emma with a wide grin. The two lawyers were looking forward to some relaxation around the Christmas holidays before returning to the grind. The workload over the last several months coupled with Emma's injury had physically and mentally drained her. She was fully aware that she had to be in top form to finish this case and ultimately win it. She expected to relax the next day, being Sunday and begin physio on her shoulder on Monday.

Emma's own bed felt good that night. Her mother and Ben had agreed to stay at her house until she returned to The Hague, probably in January.

Emma awoke the next morning feeling refreshed. The weather was unseasonably mild in Toronto so she decided to take a brisk walk in her nearby park. She was still not comfortable with jogging because of the almost constant pain in her shoulder. She was joined by a small army of armed security agents for her walk.

Ingrid was certainly taking no chances this time. She had also insisted that Emma wear a bullet-proof vest when out in public. Two agents walked in front of her and two behind. She smirked, and then mused that she was better protected than the president of the United States! She chuckled to herself and then started off with her ample security detail.

After walking for about twenty minutes in the park Emma heard a familiar male voice call to her. In a flash, four hand guns were drawn and trained on the stunned man.

Emma turned with a surprised look on her face to see her friend. "Elazar?" she asked. She raised her hand toward the agents and assured them that Elazar was not a threat.

The agents slowly holstered their weapons while their eyes remained fixed upon the man.

Emma invited her friend to sit with her on a nearby park bench. The two exchanged pleasantries for a moment and then Elazar's face took on a concerned look. "I was shocked when I learned of your ordeal, Emma. Have the authorities apprehended the guilty party?"

"Not that I am aware of," she answered.

"I am afraid that it illustrates the tenacity of the forces working against you," said Elazar.

Emma looked down with a sullen expression and said, "I'm just not sure I can continue with this, Elazar."

Elazar nodded slowly and said softly to his friend. "I understand your dilemma and I do not believe that anyone could fault you for stepping aside. But I believe that the Lord chose you for this undertaking. I am certain that this is part of His plan for you. Consider this; God could have chosen any number of attorneys for this momentous trial, but He chose Emma Collins! He knew that you are the person who had what it takes to win this battle." Elazar breathed deeply as he considered his next words. "I realize that you have been through some perilous situations; car crashes, an attempt at being run off the road and being shot! That would be too much for most people, but you have persevered. Do you understand, Emma, that that is why the Lord chose you as part of His plan?"

Emma nodded slowly as she turned to look at her friend. Elazar continued, "You are aware that time is of the essence; that the end times are quickly approaching. This is precisely what makes this trial so crucial."

For the time she had known him, Emma had held Elazar's opinions and advice in the highest regard. She had never known anyone who displayed the wisdom and insight into life, especially concerning the things of God. He continually displayed a calm, confident demeanor that caused Emma to believe that God was actually speaking through him. She hung on every word that Elazar spoke, for she felt the wisdom in his voice. Emma was starting to feel more determined and invigorated as she listened to the bearded man. She was feeling ashamed that she had considered not returning to The Hague. She felt a wave of determination rise up and pledged to herself and God that she would see this case through.

"I must say, Elazar, every time we speak I leave feeling rejuvenated! You always know the right things to say."

Elazar smiled and said, "I simply speak the truth."

With that he rose and said, "Until we meet again, Emma Collins." He nodded to his friend, straightened his weathered Aussie hat and strolled off into the distance as Emma and her security detail watched him disappear in the distance.

Emma, Heather and Ben spent a quiet Christmas together as Emma continued with her physio regimen. Tyrell and Zahra plus Jeff Bulac and his wife had joined them for an enjoyable Christmas dinner. Emma was eager to return to The Hague to continue the trial which had been set for January 17. She was feeling stronger both physically and mentally and was anxious to get back into the courtroom.

Emma could still feel the electricity in the air over the court case. Never in history had a trial created such interest and division. Emma thought back a decade to the pandemic and how it had created a similar divide in friends and families alike. That division paled in comparison to the wedges that this trial created in society. She questioned if the world would ever recover from it. *Elazar was right,* she thought to herself, *there are some powerful forces at work here.*

Emma and Tyrell spent the first two weeks of January poring over trial notes and attempting to identify any errors that they had made so far. They contacted witnesses who were slated to appear for the defense and studied their planned testimonies.

On the evening of January 14, Emma, Tyrell, and their considerable security detail boarded the Leer Jet once again at Pearson Airport. Moments later they gracefully lifted off the runway, bound for The Netherlands.

40

Monday, January 17
World Court of Justice
The Hague
9:00 am

The courtroom was as packed this morning as the proverbial can of sardines. Reporters from news agencies around the world were jostling for position. Interest at the beginning of the trial was high, but since the attempt on Emma's life it had exploded. Security in the courtroom, entire justice building and surrounding area was like nothing that the world had seen before. Metal detectors were everywhere, while armed guards, both in uniform and plain clothes, patrolled assiduously. Helicopters buzzed overhead regularly scanning the surroundings. No expense was being spared to ensure the safety of everyone involved in the trial. Emma and Tyrell had been provided a bullet-proof SUV for their trip to the courthouse and back.

A hush fell over the room as Emma and Tyrell entered surrounded by their security detail. Emma could not believe the anxiety she felt in the room. She silently prayed that God would help her overcome any feeling of apprehension as the trial resumed. The two attorneys took their seats, offering a faint smile and nod to the opposing council. They felt well prepared, better prepared than at the beginning of the trial. Once they were seated, the chatter resumed throughout the room. Emma and Tyrell opened their brief cases and quickly compared a couple of notes.

Once again the courtroom fell silent. Everyone stood as the fifteen justices filed in and took their seats behind the bench.

Chief Justice Samuel Cardoso spoke. "Welcome everyone to the resumption of the case against Christianity. We trust that another interruption will not occur." He looked at Emma and said, "Miss Collins, it is wonderful to see that you have recovered. Are you and co-counsel ready to begin?"

"Thank you, Your Honour, yes we are."

The chief justice turned his eyes toward Yankov and asked, "Mr. Yankov, is the prosecution ready to proceed?"

"We are, Your Honour."

"All right, then. Let us proceed." Both councils have been given transcripts from the beginning of the trial to bring all of you up to speed. "Miss Collins, you may begin."

"Thank you, Your Honour. Defense re-calls Doctor Caitlin Burke."

As the doctor took her seat Justice Cardoso reminded her that she is still under oath.

"Hello again, Dr. Burke," said Emma as she approached the witness stand. "Doctor Burke, we hear much about the person of Jesus of Nazareth. As a pastor and author, what can you tell us about Jesus of Nazareth?"

The doctor adjusted her microphone slightly and began to speak. "As documented by the Bible, Jesus was born in the town of Bethlehem which was about ten kilometers south of Jerusalem approximately two thousand years ago. Now, I don't think too many people doubt that Jesus actually lived. I believe the pressing question is how they view His death and resurrection. Did Jesus actually rise from the dead? So let's look at the evidence. Jesus foretold of His death and resurrection many times in the Bible. He claimed that He would be crucified and then rise again on the third day. You see, many people today are comfortable with the idea that there is a God. But when they are asked to accept that Jesus was His son…well, that's where the trouble begins. Acts 17: 31 states that 'He has given assurance of this by raising Him from the dead.' "

"How then do we know that Jesus was, in fact, raised from the dead?" asked Emma as she slowly paced with her head slightly pointed down.

"Well, let's take a look at the historical accounts of Jesus in the Bible, viewing the Bible as a historical document as we would view other historical documents. Most biblical scholars, not only evangelical but others who teach in secular universities accept the accounts of Jesus as fact. I'll give you four of these facts.

Number one: After His crucifixion Jesus was buried in a tomb by Joseph of Armathea, a member of the Jewish Sanhedrin. Now this is important because if the tomb were in a location in Jerusalem known to Jews and Christians alike, then it would be impossible to mount any movement founded on the belief in the resurrection. Basically, it would be impossible for anyone to claim that Jesus had risen from the dead, because His body was located in a tomb known to many."

"And what do scholars think of this assertion, Doctor?" asked Emma as she leaned on the witness stand.

"Most scholars recognize that the burial account of Jesus is a historical fact. There are many independent accounts verifying this account. Also, the fact that Jesus was buried by a member of the hated Sanhedrin instead of His family or His disciples is further proof on the likelihood that this story is true."

"Go on, Doctor Burke," said Emma as she stood near the witness box.

"Number two: The tomb was then discovered empty by a group of female followers on the Sunday morning after His crucifixion. Again this account is attested in independent and early sources. We have about six independent sources that attest to this account and historical events are generally considered true if we have two or more independent accounts. So with six accounts I think it is safe to say that this story is fact."

Emma asked, "Why is it significant that *women* discovered the empty tomb?"

"This is what we refer to as the 'criterion of embarrassment.' You have to understand that in first century Jewish society the testimony of women was regarded as so worthless that they wouldn't have been believed. So if someone wanted to concoct a fictitious story, they certainly would not use testimony from women. It just would not be believed. Also, the mere fact that the Jewish leaders admitted the body was gone attest to the validity of the resurrection. Instead of just denying it, they tried to make excuses for its disappearance, such as 'His disciples came at night and stole Him away while we slept.' Matthew 28:13 NKJV"

"What is the third fact, Dr. Burke"?

"Various individuals and groups experienced appearances of Jesus alive after His death. Paul states in 1st Corinthians 15: 5-8 that 'He (meaning Jesus) was seen by Cephas, then by the twelve'. He goes on to say that 'He then appeared to more than five hundred brethren at one time, most of whom are still alive. He then appeared to James and all the apostles. Then last of all He appeared also to me, Paul.' The fact that Paul states that most of these people are still alive is his invitation to seek them out to confirm what he has written. Based on how early after the resurrection this account was written, every New Testament scholar accepts it as true."

"And number four, Doctor Burke?" prompted Emma.

"The original disciples suddenly and sincerely came to believe that God raised Jesus from the dead. You see, the crucifixion of Jesus was a catastrophe for the disciples. Jewish belief was certainly not that their messiah would be crucified. They also didn't believe it was possible for Him to be resurrected so soon. They realized that God had indeed raised Jesus from the dead after their encounters with Him. This extraordinary transformation of the disciples only goes to prove the validity of the resurrection. So if you consider these four facts, then we have no choice but to accept that Jesus did rise from the dead and that He is truly the Son of God."

Thank you, Dr. Burke. No further questions."

"Does the prosecution have any questions for this witness?" asked the chief justice as he made some brief notations.

"No, Your Honour," replied Yankov.

"You may step down, Doctor. You may call the next witness."

"The defense calls Dr. Meredith Lee."

"Dr. Lee, please state your occupation," asked Emma as she stood and approached the witness stand.

Doctor Lee was in her mid-fifties. She was fashionably dressed in a pale-yellow dress with a light brown jacket. "I am a history professor at Yale University. I specialize in ancient history. I have also written several books on ancient Rome and the Religious establishment during that time in history."

Emma thought for a moment and then said, "Dr. Lee, we have heard biblical testimony that Jesus did, in fact, certainly exist. In your research Doctor, is there any ***non*** biblical evidence supporting these claims?"

"Absolutely! Actually there is more evidence for Jesus than almost any other famous or important person of that time. For example, Cornelius Tacitus, considered one of the greatest historians of Rome at that time, lived from 55 to 120 A.D. He wrote that 'Christ, who was the founder of Christianity, was put to death by Pontius Pilate.' His writings went on to confirm five things; that Jesus did exist, that He was the founder of Christianity, that He was put to death by Pontius Pilate, that Christianity originated in Judea and that later it spread to Rome."

"But Dr. Lee," inquired Emma, "could Tacitus have just gotten his information from Christian sources?"

"Not likely. As a historian, he would have looked at sources such as government records instead of Christian testimony. He certainly would not have wanted a Christian slant on any of his research. Also, in his writings he always distinguished between confirmed information and hearsay. There is no mention of hearsay in his writings about Jesus. So we have to conclude that his information was accurate. And bear in mind, Tacitus was not a Christian. His writings indicate he actually did not believe Jesus to be the Son of God. So he had no other reason to talk about Jesus than simply the fact that Jesus *did* exist and was important to many people. He just wrote the facts as he saw them."

"Is it possible that his writings could have been tampered with over the years in favour of Christianity?"

"I see no evidence of tampering in any of his writings. They all seem to be consistent."

"Now Dr. Lee, what other evidence is there?" asked Emma.

"Well, another reliable source is the early Greek satirist, Lucian of Samasata. He described at length his views of Christianity and actually ridiculed Christianity and Christ. Now, his writings confirm that Jesus was the founder of Christianity and was crucified. Allow me to read from the writings of Lucian. 'The Christians, you know, worship a man to this day – the distinguished personage who introduced their novel rite, and was crucified on that account…It was impressed on them by their original law giver that they are all brothers from the moment they are converted and deny the gods of Greece and worship the crucified sage, and live after his laws…'

Now this passage was translated into old English, but we can understand it to confirm that Jesus did exist; He was the founder of Christianity and was worshipped by His followers and was crucified."

Emma turned to the members of the court. She was trying to

gauge how receptive they were to the testimony, so far. "How do we know that this is reliable?" she asked.

"Again, Lucian believed that his task was to tell it as it happened… to eliminate anything that was untrue. He often criticized his contemporaries for injecting their beliefs into their writings. Also, Lucian mocked Jesus and Christianity so he had no reason to alter the events in his writings. He would certainly stick to the facts. So yes, that tells us that his accounts would be totally reliable."

"Is there any other non biblical confirmation of the existence of Jesus?" Emma queried.

"Yes, there is. The Romano – Jewish historian Flavius Josephus wrote from 94 – 95 A.D. speaking of the crucifixion of Jesus, 'but his brother James who was stoned to death and the imprisonment and death of John the Baptist.' He writes that he considered Christianity a 'dangerous superstition'. So again, the writings of Josephus prove that Jesus did exist, He founded Christianity, had many followers, had a brother named James and was put to death under Pontius Pilate. Also, a man by the name of Pliny the Younger was a Roman governor who in 112 A.D. sent a letter to Emperor Trajan to ask how he should deal with Christians. Pliny was attempting to halt the spread of Christianity. And I quote 'They sing to Christ as if He were a god'. End quote. He explained in his writings that he would give the people accused of following Christ the chance to renounce Christ and worship the Roman gods or be put to death. Pliny noted an underlying trend that those who truly believed in the Christ were willing to die for their beliefs. Let me read an excerpt from one of Pliny's letters concerning Christians. Christians were, quote *'meeting on a certain fixed day before it was light, when they sang an alternate verse a hymn to Christ as to a god, and bound themselves to a solemn oath, not to do wicked deeds, never commit fraud, theft, adultery, not to lie nor to deny a trust…'*

So again we see that the writings of Pliny confirm that early Christians met together weekly, they sang songs to Jesus, they followed Jesus and were committed to a holy life. This is further recorded evidence of the existence of Jesus. Because once again, Pliny was certainly not a Christian, so he had absolutely *no* reason to invent such a story."

Emma sounded confident as she said to Yankov, "Your witness."

Yankov remained seated and said mockingly, "Doctor Lee, how can we be sure that these writings are actually authentic? How do these alleged writings prove *anything?*"

"Well sir, written history is the only way to *prove* historical events from long ago. For example, I would guess that every person in this room believes Alexander the Great existed; but no one here ever *saw* him, did they? We only have written records to prove that Alexander the Great did in fact, exist. And as a matter of fact, no accounts of Alexander the Great were written until five hundred years after his death. In comparison, some accounts of Jesus were written within a few years of His crucifixion. An example of that is original pieces of the book of Matthew which date back to just a few years after the death of Christ. So why then should we not believe the accounts of Jesus?"

Yankov found himself lost for words. "Uh, I have no further questions for this witness, Your Honour."

The doctor continued, "And also, you must understand…"

"No further questions!" cried Yankov. He could feel that the trial was slipping away and it frightened him. This is certainly not the way he expected the trial to unfold.

Yankov's next witness was Doctor Alina Bauer. Doctor Bauer was a renowned author with a doctorate in philosophy from the University of Munich. She had studied the claim of Christians that Jesus of Nazareth was the Son of God.

Doctor Bauer was an elegant woman in her mid-forties. She was smartly dressed in a two-piece black business suit with an attractive red, blue and black blouse. The doctor had an unmistakable air of confidence about her as she made her way to the witness box.

Miroslav Yankov smiled broadly as he approached his witness. This was the witness who he believed could win the case for him.

"Doctor Bauer is it true that you have studied the subject of Jesus thoroughly over your career?" began Yankov.

"Yes, that is true. I have spent years poring over the facts concerning the claim that Jesus is God."

"And what conclusion did you reach, Doctor?" asked Yankov as he looked back at the onlookers in the court room.

"After years of study it is clear to me that Jesus was absolutely *not* God."

"Please explain," replied Yankov, feeling more confident by the second.

"I will give six reasons to prove my findings:

Number one: The Bible states that Jesus was physically born of a mortal woman. '…Mary, of whom was born Jesus who is called Christ.' Matthew 1:16 NKJV. If He were God, then that is impossible. God is eternal, so He could never have been born, let alone to a human mother.

Number two: Jesus claimed to be God and human at the same time. Again, this is absurd. He was human, so therefore he could not possibly also be God. God cannot be contained in human form.

Number three: The Trinity that the Bible talks about. This idea of the trinity, the Father, Son and Holy Spirit didn't come about until the third century. Had the trinity been real, then Jesus would have talked about it.

Number four: God is self sufficient. Jesus was not. Jesus needed to eat and sleep as a human in order to live. He also prayed to God, which begs the question, *(She hold hands out palms up)* why would he pray to himself? Of course, he wouldn't if he were God, so obviously he was *not* God.

Number five: Jesus claimed that he didn't know when he would return, that only God did. So again, he admits he was not God.

Number six: He admitted that the Father was greater than He. He states that in the book of John that "I am going to the Father, for my Father is greater than I. Again, this goes to prove that He was not God."

"So again, Doctor, what conclusions can we draw from these facts?"

"Clearly that Jesus was not God. Time and time again, what he said and what he did proved contrary to him being God."

Yankov set his gaze upon the panel of judges as he put the next question to Doctor Bauer.

"Now, Dr. Bauer, when we consider Christianity today, what in your expert opinion, is the effect that it is having on society?"

"In my view, the actual consequence of Christianity in society is a bigger problem than most realize."

"Please expand on that, Doctor."

"Well, let's examine history and consider such events as the Crusades a thousand years ago. We have to wonder how these atrocities could have been committed in the name of Christ, if in fact, Jesus was peace loving. Too many wars have been waged in Christ's name throughout history.

Now we come to the subject of the effect that Christianity is having on today's modern culture. It seems to me that Christians want to stymie any progression of modern society."

"Tell the court what you mean by that, Doctor."

"Time and time again when society needs to advance in a sociological manner, Christians mount a fierce effort to thwart it. An example of this is the subject of abortion. Christians believe that a woman should not have a choice in this matter; that she should not have control over her own body. This is *clearly* holding back the progression of a modern society."

"Thank you Doctor. No further questions," said Yankov as he returned to his seat with a smug look on his face.

"Cross, Your Honour?" said Emma as she jumped to her feet.

"Of course," answered the chief justice as he wrote down a couple of notations.

"Doctor Bauer, you told this court that in your view Christians are 'un- progressive' to consider the murder of unborn babies wrong. Did you not?"

"Objection! Your Honour, my witness said no such thing!" bellowed Yankov.

"Your Honour, Dr. Bauer certainly did say that she was comfortable with abortion. She criticized Christians for being *against* it!" explained Emma fervently.

"She did not use the word *murder*, Your Honour!" said Yankov heatedly.

Emma glared at her opponent "Terminating pregnancies! What else should we call it?"

"That's enough from both of you!" chided Chief Justice Cardoso. "Both councils approach the bench. Ms. Collins, you *will* use a better choice of words in the future cross-examinations or face a charge of contempt. Am I clear?"

Emma realized that she had allowed Yankov to rattle her and vowed that she would not fall into that trap again. "My apologies, Your Honour."

"Step back and continue," hissed the judge.

"I have no further questions for this witness, Your Honour," said Emma as she returned to her seat.

"The defense would like to recall Dr. Lucas Balaskas to the stand," said Emma.

After the witness had settled into his seat Emma began, "Dr. Balaskas, what do you say in response to the previous witness's claims that Christianity has been responsible for so many of the world's wars and the genocide of millions?"

"I understand that this is a commonly held belief by many. But let's examine the facts. In the twentieth century, there were far more atrocities committed than ever before. It is said that Chairman Moa Zedong was responsible for the mass murder of as many as sixty million people. Joseph Stalin, who in his earlier days was attending a seminary; He later renounced God and went on to be responsible for the deaths of an estimated fifteen million people. Hitler and Lenin committed atrocities resulting in millions more dying. So to say that most of the atrocities were committed by Christians is just not true.

Now, when dealing with historical wars waged in the name of religion, we have to ask ourselves, is the person perpetrating these horrific acts keeping with his religion, or is he in violation of it? When Jesus was captured by Roman soldiers, He could have repelled them by violence. At any time during His beatings and subsequent crucifixion, He could have used violence to end it. But He did not. In *fact,* while He was being crucified He was heard to say 'Father forgive them, for they do not know what they do.' Luke 23:34 NKJV. Now, I ask you, does this sound like a man committed to violence?

So it becomes a philosophical question. Murder is a violation of Christianity. But an atheist *could* commit murder and be keeping with his philosophy. Of course, I'm not saying that all atheists are murderers. What I am saying is that an atheist *could* commit such a crime and actually be in tune with his philosophy; as demented as that philosophy might be. So in the case of so called Christians committing atrocities, we should never judge a religion by its abuse. We should judge it only by its merits."

Emma continued, "Doctor Balaskas, the prosecution's last witness stated several reasons why she believes Jesus was not God. How do you respond to these assertions?"

"There are many instances in the Bible that prove that Jesus was God. I shall mention a few. First of all, we must understand that Jesus had two distinct natures; He was 100% human and 100% divine. This means that Jesus is both man and God. He did not lose His divinity when He became a man. He could have stopped His crucifixion, but He knew that being sacrificed for our sins was His purpose on earth. Let me give you some examples of the Bible proving that Jesus was God.

1. God never changes…Malachi 3:6 says, For I am the Lord, I do not change.

   Jesus never changes…Hebrews 13:8 says 'Jesus Christ is the same yesterday, today and forever.'

2. God is our Savior…Isaiah 43:11 I, even I am the Lord, and besides Me there is no Savior.

   Jesus is our Savior…Acts 4: 12…Nor is there salvation in any other, for there is no other name under heaven given among men by which we must be saved.

3. God created the universe…Genesis 1:1 In the beginning God created the heavens and the earth.

   Jesus created the universe…John 1:3…In the beginning was the Word, and the Word was with God, and the Word was God. All things were made through Him, and without Him nothing was made that was made.

4. God forgives sin…Mark 2:7…Who can forgive sins but God alone?

   Jesus forgives sin…Colossians 1:14 in whom we have redemption through His blood, the forgiveness of sins.

You see, there are many, many scriptures that confirm that Jesus is God. I've mentioned just a few. Again, we must understand that Jesus was 100% man *and* 100% divine."

"Thank you. No further questions," said Emma.

"You may step down," said the chief justice. "The prosecution may call the next witness."

"The prosecution rests, Your Honour."

"The defense rests, Your Honour."

"Very well, then. Court is adjourned until next Monday morning for closing arguments." Chief Justice Cardoso banged his gavel loudly.

The courtroom again buzzed with anticipation as reporters jostled to exit in order to file their stories and others began debating the possible outcomes of the trial.

As Yankov and his co-council were packing their brief cases they were approached by the Secretary of the U.N., Victor Morozov. Morozov was obviously in a foul mood as he approached the two attorneys.

"What is going on, Miroslav?" he asked in a bitter tone.

"Sir?"

"You are losing this case! That is what is going on! You assured me of an easy victory," added Morozov, seething with anger.

Hendrickson was shaking with fear as he attempted to plead their case, "Mr. Secretary General, our witnesses are not performing as we expected. They assured us that their testimonies would be sufficient to easily win this case."

Victor Morozov went into a rage. "You two indicated that you would have a stacked deck of expert witnesses. Well, gentlemen, your house of cards is about to collapse on top of the two of you if you do not find a way to win this case. And that defense attorney, she's barely thirty years old! But she is making the two of you look like law students! I warn you two, your closing statement had better be sufficient to turn the tide on this case." Morozov turned and stormed out of the courtroom as his two attorneys stood with a look of dismay on their faces.

Emma and Tyrell had witnessed part of the exchange which increased their confidence level of the outcome of the case.

"Okay," said Emma as she exhaled loudly, "We have a week to prepare our close. Let's get at it." They finished packing their brief cases and exited the courtroom, surrounded once again by their security detail.

January 31

Emma and Tyrell entered the courtroom again under intense security. The room was noticeably quieter than the previous week. Emma sensed that there was a nervous anticipation in the room. The tension in the room was palpable. A decision would be rendered shortly that would undoubtedly set a course for humankind for the rest of time. Ramifications from the ruling would resonate throughout the entire world.

"Are both counsels ready for closing remarks?" asked the chief justice.

Both counsels acknowledged their readiness.

"Very well, prosecution may proceed."

Miroslav Yankov rose and walked in the direction of the panel of judges. He was acutely aware that his career was riding on his performance today. The secretary general had made that fact abundantly clear. He had originally believed that this assignment would propel him to greater heights. Now he was not so sure. He had underestimated Emma Collins and this was his final opportunity to salvage this case and his future.

"Chief Justice and esteemed members of the court," began Yankov, "we have heard endless testimony from an array of defense witnesses in this case. If nothing else, it has been totally confusing! Defense counsel talks of three Gods…and one God… I'm not quite sure if they themselves know what to believe! We live in an age where we have left superstition and false hope in an unseen God behind us. We belong to a modern, progressive society. We understand that we don't need a make believe God or antiquated book to guide our society. Our society will be guided by our human morality. We only have to believe in ourselves and our governments.

Now, the defense has presented a noble case, very eloquently, I might add. But I fear it has no substance. They prattle on about humankind being unable to chart our own destinies. They claim that without their God we are doomed. But, Your Honours, look around; our society is doing just fine! We do of course, have our challenges, but for the most part we have always been able to overcome these challenges. Again, our human morality will always see us through.

Now as members of this jury, you have been given the extraordinary opportunity to help set the course for the future of humankind. So…it is incumbent upon you to find in favour of the prosecution and allow this society to ban Christianity and rid the world of this dysfunctional religion. Thank you."

Yankov returned to his seat, confident in his closing remarks.

"Miss Collins?" said the chief justice.

Emma rose slowly and looked directly at the chief justice. "Thank you, Your Honour." Emma felt the pressure building as she realized that this entire case and the future of Christianity being legal was riding on her summation. She silently prayed that God would strengthen her and calm her nerves. She approached the panel of judges and began.

"Chief Justice, Your Honours; You are charged today with making a monumental decision. The decision of arriving at a verdict of 'yes' or 'no'…Yes, to a world wide ban on Christianity or no, that Christianity be allowed to exist and flourish throughout the world. A verdict, Your Honours that will have *profound* ramifications all over the globe. Over the course of this trial, you have been inundated with a barrage of facts and opinions. The prosecution has used a plethora of opinions and assumptions disguised as facts to argue their case. They have paraded various scholars and well educated witnesses in front of you, endeavouring to persuade you with a lot of gibberish simply because their case is weak! On the flip side, the defense has elected to use *facts* to argue on the side of Christianity. Now, *we* could have talked endlessly about the love, compassion, the saving power and faithfulness of Christ, but we chose instead to stick to facts in defense of this challenge. Although all these qualities of Christ are true, this being a court of law, we opted for a factual defense."

Emma continued, "Now ladies and gentlemen, the defense has presented the facts to you in this case, beginning with the existence of God. Whether we speak of the 'fine tuning of the universe' or the 'wonder of the human body's thirty to forty *trillion* cells and extremely complex DNA codes', we have no alternative but to accept that these extraordinary scientific facts are the result of an intelligence *far* beyond our comprehension. And that intelligence, of course, is none other than God himself. We have heard all the feeble arguments trying to explain the origin of life." Emma paused for effect. "But upon closer scrutiny, we have to concede that these arguments, such as a universe that just 'happened by chance' just *do not* make any sense. For any mind, scientific or not, *God* is the only plausible explanation.

We next contemplated the existence of Jesus. Now, with the exhaustive research of our witnesses, there is no doubt that Jesus was born, lived, was crucified, and rose from the dead. The evidence is just *too* overwhelming to deny it. Historical records substantiate Christ's claim of deity. As you all can now attest to the volume of evidence is astounding. Our witnesses also debunked the notion that true Christianity was cause of most wars throughout history. As was presented into evidence, far more bloodshed and atrocities were committed by atheists than were committed in the name of Christ.

Now ladies and gentlemen, what we did not include in our defense, were the intangibles. We did not include the love of Jesus, the compassion that He shows; His faithfulness and His saving power, just to mention a few. These traits of Jesus are known to us through a personal relationship with Him. Without these wonderful attributes of Jesus, the world would be a much darker place. Let me read a quote from the world renowned Christian apologist, the late Ravi Zacharias." Tyrell handed her a paper. "And I quote, 'He (meaning God) is the only entity in existence that the reason for being is in Himself. All other entities exist by virtue of something else. And in that sense *He* is perfect.' Emma handed the paper back to Tyrell. "So…we have a perfect God and of course a perfect Jesus. Now, are Christians perfect? No, but we have that perfect example to imitate.

So, Your Honours, you have a choice. Do you decide to ban Christianity and rid the world of the one *true* God? Do you want a darker, more corrupt world? Or, do you want Christianity to continue to grow and flourish? Do you want to allow this world to receive the love and compassion from our Saviour, Jesus Christ? Do you want a world where we are free to follow the King of kings? Do you want a world free of tyranny? A world in which we are free to receive eternal life from God?" Emma paused for effect. "I trust you will choose to strike down this proposed ban. You must… for all of our sakes. Thank you."

Emma returned to her seat; she felt drained. She had put everything into her closing remarks and felt that she had nothing left to give. Tyrell placed his hand on her shoulder and whispered, "That was brilliant, girl!"

Emma smiled faintly, took a deep breath and exhaled loudly, relieved that it was over. Much testimony had been offered on both sides of the argument and now it was finally concluded. Emma silently prayed that she had argued the case for Christianity successfully. She believed she had done her best and now decided to leave it up to God.

The fifteen justices convened quietly for a few moments and then Chief Justice Cardoso spoke. "Thank you counsellors for your arguments. The court will convene and render our verdict in due time. This court is adjourned." With that said the justices rose and exited to their chambers.

Emma and Tyrell shouldered their way through the courtroom toward the rear exit. Their security detail cleared a path through the throngs of spectators and news people. The two were ushered into their waiting vehicle and whisked away to their hotel to await the verdict. It had been a stressful few weeks and months for them and now they must patiently await the verdict. *What would happen if they won? What would happen if they lost?* Emma considered both scenarios and was somewhat fearful of either. People were so divided and she wondered how the world would move on from it.

Emma and Tyrell met in the hotel restaurant later for dinner and discussed the trial and possible outcomes. Either way, they were excited at the prospect of returning home and back to their relatively normal lives. After dinner they met in a quiet section of the hotel lobby and quietly prayed for the outcome of the trial and the reverberations that it would cause throughout the world.

42

The call from Ingrid came four days later to inform Emma that the court had arrived at a verdict. A vehicle would pick them up shortly and drive them to the court house.

There was an eerie silence as Emma and Tyrell entered the courtroom. The mood seemed tense, a stark difference from a few days earlier.

Emma and Tyrell took their seats and waited. Moments later the fifteen justices filed in. A hush fell upon the courtroom. Chief Justice Cardoso adjusted his microphone and then began. "The past several weeks have been unlike anything this court has ever witnessed. This was an unusual case in the sense that no crime had actually been committed. It was more of a grievance of sorts filed by a number of nations of the world. The allegations against the Christian religion throughout the world are serious. Christianity has been labelled by the prosecution as a false and dangerous religion that should be banned for the sake of the entire world. The defense argued that Christianity is the one true religion and is necessary for the well-being of the planet. The court has studied these arguments and discussed both sides at length. It is generally the position of the court to refrain from involving itself in religious matters. Although, in this particular case, the sheer number of grievances and complaints against Christianity prompted the court to make an exception. In studying this case, the court examined the argument from both sides and made its decision based on the testimony and what is in the best interest of the people of the world. Therefore, the decision of this court is that Christianity should *not* be banned. To ban this religion, the court believes, would be a monumental misstep. This court is adjourned." With that, the chief justice banged his gavel prompting the judges to rise and exit the courtroom.

The courtroom erupted in deafening noise. Half of the spectators cheered wildly while the other half protested vehemently. Tyrell and Emma looked at each other and then embraced. Once again their security detail quickly escorted them from the courthouse to their awaiting vehicle.

As they drove back to their hotel they were slowed by protesters who were already making their displeasure with the ruling known.

Upon arrival at their hotel, Emma and Tyrell were whisked in through a rear entrance. Protesters in front of the hotel were making it almost impossible to enter through the main doors. They finally were able to escape the crowds and take sanctuary in their secure hotel rooms.

The following morning Tyrell joined Emma for breakfast. They decided for safety reasons to order room service rather than risk going to a restaurant. They were scheduled to meet with Ingrid and Reverend Nordstrom at 11 am and then drive to the airport where the Leer would be waiting for them.

After breakfast Emma and Tyrell packed their suitcases and then were escorted to their awaiting vehicle. When they stepped outside they were stunned at the damage that had been inflicted on the city by the rioters. Emma stared in disbelief at the carnage all around her. Hundreds of broken windows, over-turned and burned cars and even buildings still ablaze were etched into her mind.

"Ma'am, let's hurry," said one of her security agents rather forcefully as he directed his two charges into the awaiting SUV.

They drove off through the debris-filled streets as quickly as they were able.

Thirty minutes later they arrived at Ingrid Swenson's office and were greeted by Ingrid and Reverend Nordstrom. The office was not well known so it had not attracted any protesters.

"Good morning to you both," said Ingrid with a smile as she met them at the door. "Reverend Nordstrom is inside." She led them into a separate room where the reverend was seated.

Nordstrom rose from his seat and greeted them warmly with a smile and hand shake.

After they were seated Nordstrom began, "I wanted to meet with the two of you this morning to express our gratitude in all that you accomplished in this court case. Ingrid and I thank you on behalf of the Council of Churches and all Christians throughout the world. I know you must be wondering what good you did in light of all the riots last night, but the fact of the matter is that if you had lost the case churches would have been forced underground all over the world. That would have prevented many people from coming to know Christ. Both of you were exemplary in your handling of this case and we are proud to have had you with us."

"Thank you, Reverend for the kind words. It was our pleasure to work on behalf of our Lord," said Emma.

"Now, Ingrid tells me that the balance of your stipend has been deposited into your accounts along with a well-deserved bonus. Now, continued the reverend, you must both be anxious to return home, so the jet is at your disposal and is waiting for you at the airport."

"Thank you both," said Tyrell as they rose and shook hands with Ingrid and Nordstrom.

Emma and Tyrell were once again ushered into their vehicle and whisked away to Schiphol airport. The jet was already running when they arrived and they were in the air within minutes on their way back to Toronto.

As the Leer rose through the clouds, Emma stared out at the darkening winter sky with mixed feelings. She was relieved that they had won the case, but saddened at the chaos that had ensued afterwards. She prayed for the people of the world who did not know Christ. She prayed for a healing of the troubled hearts of the world. She knew in her own heart that God was in control and that He would work things out. She thanked Him for using her as part of *His Plan*.

The End

Author's Note:

This book is a work of fiction. It is based on possible events as the world grows closer to the end-times. The Bible states that Christ will return to the earth once again and eventually this earth will be no more. *"And this gospel of the kingdom will be preached in all the world as a witness to all the nations, and then the* ***end*** *will come."* Matthew 24:14

If you read this book and have never accepted Christ as your saviour, then now is the time. Just simply reach out to Him. He will forgive any sins in your life and give you a place in Heaven.

Blessings!
Miles R. Wilson

Acknowledgments

New King James Bible © 1982 Thomas Nelson

Did Jesus Rise From the Dead? © 2014 Dr. William Lane Craig

How Did Life Begin? © 2011 Stephen Hawking

John Lennox (2012)

Ravi Zacharias Ministries Toronto, Canada Atlanta, USA